Seasons of Purgatory

Seasons
of
Purgatory

ooooo

Shahriar Mandanipour

Translated from the Persian by
Sara Khalili

Bellevue Literary Press
New York

First published in the United States in 2022
by Bellevue Literary Press, New York
For information, contact:
Bellevue Literary Press
90 Broad Street
Suite 2100
New York, NY 10004
www.blpress.org

Library of Congress Cataloging-in-Publication Data
Names: Mandanī'pūr, Shahriyār, author. | Khalili, Sara, translator.
Title: Seasons of purgatory / Shahriar Mandanipour ; translated from the
Persian by Sara Khalili.
Description: First edition. | New York : Bellevue Literary Press, 2022.
Identifiers: LCCN 2021001686 | ISBN 9781942658955 (paperback) |
ISBN 9781942658962 (epub)
Subjects: LCSH: Mandanī'pūr, Shahriyār--Translations into English.
Classification: LCC PK6561.M236 A2 2022 | DDC 891/.5533--dc23
LC record available at https://lccn.loc.gov/2021001686

Bellevue Literary Press would like to thank all its generous
donors—individuals and foundations—for their support.

 This publication is made possible by the New York State
Council on the Arts with the support of the Office of the
Governor and the New York State Legislature.

Book design and composition by Mulberry Tree Press, Inc.

Bellevue Literary Press is committed to ecological stewardship in our
book production practices, working to reduce our impact on the natural
environment.

♾ This book is printed on acid-free paper.

Manufactured in the United States of America.

First Edition

1   3   5   7   9   8   6   4   2

paperback ISBN: 978-1-942658-95-5
ebook ISBN: 978-1-942658-96-2

To Baran and Danial,
who have brought me joy in one hand
and hope in the other.

Contents

Seasons of Purgatory

Shadows of the Cave

M R. FARVANEH SAID, "Let's assume it isn't so. But
don't be surprised if one day you see a vulture
of the bald species sitting on the edge of the trash can
in your kitchen, excavating it." And then he talked
about that old lion and how it was no coincidence that
in these types of nightmares, and even in our wakeful
hours, any lion we imagine is old and weary. "If you
prefer, you can roll over in bed and think of the few
hours of sleep left until morning. But if you half rise
on your elbows and look, you will see that the lion has
rested his paws on the edge of your bed and is staring
at you with his sleepy eyes. The magnificent halo of his
reddish brown mane is unforgettable, and he looks as if
he has just smelled an unpleasant odor for the very first
time, which has caused his cheeks to pucker like that."

Apart from his occasional ill temper, Mr. Farvaneh
was a pleasant talker and possessed exceptional powers
of depiction and analysis. In the bakery, he could be
singled out for the way he stood on line sideways, perhaps because of his dread of coming into contact with
others, or in the morning, for the one bottle of milk
and the one pack of cigarettes he carried as he climbed
the stairs up to his apartment. If you were rushed in
greeting him and did so in passing, he would pretend

not to have noticed you at all, but the moment you stopped and talked, for example about the spread of that mysterious smell, he would undoubtedly open up to you and begin to explain his frightening theories in detail. And, finally, with perplexity and sorrow in his eyes and a smirk rife with insight into people's hidden thoughts on his lips, he would again warn, "All of us who live in this neighborhood and in this city are in danger, a danger far greater than the Mongol invasion and our massacre at their hands."

Mr. Farvaneh was an admirable man, because of his infinite knowledge in all fields of science, the fruit of years of reading and research, and because it is said that in the years preceding the 1953 coup d'état he had held a key government position. It was only after the page turned in the book of times that he took to a secluded corner, or was obliged to do so. Consequently, he was regarded as a man worthy of attention. However, as one would expect, he seldom allowed strangers to enter the sacred confines of his home. From time to time, it occurred that the midday nap or early-evening slumber of the residents of our apartment building was broken by his shouts of "Get out of my house," and then someone, in shock and anger, would slam the door to his apartment and descend the staircase. But there were also occasions, though not many, when neighbors or relatives would for hours delight in his company, replete with humor and engaging pleasantries.

Mr. Farvaneh believed that man is a pitiable two-dimensional creature with one half of his being

inclined toward a societal life and the other half pre-
ferring the sanctuary of instinctive isolationism. He
said, "Well, what does society imply? Man faced with a
done deal, just that." And perhaps to avoid such prim-
itive circumstances, he had chosen heavy curtains for
the windows in his apartment, plain and dark, which
together with light from a floor lamp created a multi-
faceted space of light and shadows. He would sink
into this somber velveteen space and drown in distant,
protracted thoughts. But suddenly, he would leap up
in a panic and light incense so that its scent would
engulf the apartment and infiltrate the stairway from
the gap beneath the front door.

One day, three or four years ago, Mr. Farvaneh
told one of the neighbors, "The presence of the smell
of animals is by no means accidental. It is most certainly deliberate. There is a purpose to it. They are not
as odorous as this. However, as long as it is written in
their destiny that they must endure the cage, this is
the only means by which they can flaunt their presence. This is the prelude to an inevitable historic battle, ominous and void of human principles. Therefore,
for the sake of the sanctity of our living environment,
we must take action and fight against this odor by any
means possible. I believe the entire populace, from
those pious-looking birds to that aged rhinoceros, has
conspired to make its scent more pungent and offen-
sive to us. They are fully aware of their effect." No one,
of course, took the last segment of Mr. Farvaneh's
comments seriously, and given their previous failed

attempt at a neighborhood petition, they all preferred to get used to the smell, and they did. They only noticed the odor on occasions when he would pontificate about it on the staircase and they, with innocent nods, would endorse the need for decisive action.

"Gradually, they will make us addicted to the conditions they have imposed on us. Little by little, and in the end . . . disease! Never would I intentionally strike fear in you, but from the commingling of the incompatible lifestyles of so many different creatures—I take us into account, as well—a new disease will undoubtedly emerge. Who knows what? A contagious and unpreventable illness that could result in the extinction of humankind, and I am sure they will all be immune to it. Why all of them? Because after years of coexistence, they have developed a cunning collective instinct. I declare a state of danger."

And in the end, Mr. Farvaneh discovered that man is a lonely, helpless creature, condemned to being misunderstood. Imagining him on the dreary days of this city, standing for hours behind a window and staring at rows of cages and the ghosts huddled inside them, would wrench the heart of any friend of the noble sons of our land, especially when the winter drizzle fell from eternally dark clouds. He couldn't spend all his time reading, preparing a simple lunch and dinner didn't take up much time, and washing his clothes, ironing, and polishing his shoes were no match for the remaining obstinate hours of the day. Mr. Farvaneh told one of the neighbors, who by chance was accompanying him on his return from a summer-afternoon stroll, "I am tired," or something to that effect, and of course he didn't mean tired from walking. He was referring to something far more profound and inclusive of mankind. He had then sighed, rubbed his hands together, and stared into the distance, far away. Perhaps he had talked about his insomnia. It is rumored among his neighbors that he barely slept three hours a night. It is natural that in old age one needs less sleep, and Mr. Farvaneh was well over sixty-five. Lamps that remain lit in an apartment throughout the night could at first pique one's curiosity, but not for long. Perhaps he slept with the lights on, most likely because light alleviates loneliness and could be considered a companion, or because he was afraid. But no, it's hard to imagine an old man afraid of the dark. According to one of the people Mr. Farvaneh spoke to—the bookseller who has a small stall across the street and stocks up on books that suit the taste of his regular clients—Mr. Farvaneh found that in the quiet and still hours of the night, no book was as satisfying as a book on history. He believed that imagining the majesty of ancient times from the comfort of an old cozy armchair made one long for unattainable glory; of course, if the howls of the hyenas copulating and the hoots of the owl that even in a cage hadn't forgotten its nightly vigil would permit. One can understand Mr. Farvaneh's agony. Isn't it true that there is no place for animals in history, except for a small niche for horses and elephants as mounts and as elements that define the geographic diversity of commanders who preferred one over the other? How one yearns for the long-lost silence of their forebearers when today curtains, even heavy curtains, cannot stop the covetous call of the male ape from infiltrating a small apartment overlooking the zoo. Mr. Farvaneh closed the book, raised his head, and gazed at the window. The shadows cast by the old lamp next to him created melancholic images on the curtains. How wide is a bark's scope of sound, for example the bark of a baboon? And then the wolves would start, especially if it was wintertime and if there was a full moon. Perhaps they saw Mr. Farvaneh's lit window. In the silent nights of the city, every call seeks a listener, and behind that window . . .

"I can hardly tolerate it. I pace up and down until I think they have fallen asleep, and only then do I find some peace and relax in my armchair. That dear departed lady offered me this armchair, and this desk and lamp, so that I would have a suitable corner to read. But every time I sit down to read a few lines, I have barely made myself comfortable when another one of them starts. I'm afraid it may not really be them. How can I tell in the dark of the night? After all these years of coexistence in a manner that would not have been possible in any jungle or desert, perhaps they have learned to mimic one another's sound. Or perhaps their howls have grown so similar that . . ." that not everyone could tell whether it was now an owl or a hyena or a monkey or a wolf or just that old parrot with the flaking beak. According to the bookseller, whom Mr. Farvaneh visited with the excuse that he might have received new merchandise, Mr. Farvaneh had found, purchased, and read all the books available on animals and their habits and behavior several years ago. Those who visited his apartment would see the collection sitting on a shelf set apart from his library and arranged in the same order as the animal cages facing his window. And there was a pair of hunting binoculars, with ample magnification, hanging beside the window. Mr. Farvaneh had a complicated allegory for animals: "If you realize that people are mocking you, and you behave in such a way that they remain ignorant of your realization, and especially if you repeat the cause of their mockery, it is, in fact, you who has mocked them and who has the upper hand. These animals use the same intelligent ploy; with only a few exceptions, in their cage they behave as they would in the jungle. At times, their indifference to humans is truly insulting. Don't you understand?" No! Many didn't grasp this fine point, or they didn't want to. Perhaps if they had had a better view and a better opportunity, the situation would have been different. For example, if they had had a window overlooking the zoo, a pair of hunting binoculars, and a comfortable chair, and they could sit for hours at a time with their elbows resting on the windowsill, at dawn, on rainy days when visitors were not blocking the view of the cages, or on moonlit nights when the ghosts with their vulgar cries called out to one another.

"I catch them off guard from my hiding place. They don't know they're being watched. It's just like hunting, but far more personal. Have you seen that elephant?

Take notice of him. He is large enough that you won't need binoculars. He defies and mocks us with his patience and poise. I personally don't believe there is any need for his shackle. He won't go anywhere; he just stands there. They always take the children up on a ladder to sit on him and take pictures, and this way . . . What occupation could be better than this? Imagine, in how many photo albums has he been immortalized?"

In fact, Mr. Farvaneh believed in nature minus the beasts. He believed that man has achieved such progress, prosperity, and self-sufficiency that he no longer has any need for the animal kingdom. "Today, the vital resources that animals squander far outweigh what they can offer." He held his cigarette butt between two fingers until the end of the discussion, when he could walk over to the trash can at the foot of the stairs. In view of these observations, and the fact that he always had something to say, Mr. Farvaneh was a man who yearned to be at the center of attention: to stand at the podium in large halls amid the enthusiastic applause of the audience, to appear on television, and to have periodicals dedicate lengthy articles to his intellect and excellence.

But surely Mr. Farvaneh was disgusted by all this. One did not see his unhappy face anywhere other than at a window overlooking the zoo. And there stood a man who, according to his wife—of course when she was alive—one day had gotten caught in a trap like a high-flying eagle. A trap that all the crows and vultures, even the most stupid among them, had escaped.

And although his incarceration after the coup d'état was very brief and he was unexpectedly released, or he somehow delivered what was required for him to secure his own release, those thirty or forty nights of detention, surrounded by cement walls, behind steel bars, and listening to execution bullets being fired outside, had resulted in astonishing changes in his beliefs and opinions. It was as if a phoenix had risen from the ashes of the man he once was.

Mr. Farvaneh didn't like to talk about his past, which was always at the center of everyone's curiosity and had somehow gained him their highest respect. His loathing for meaningless words and his disgust of having to state the obvious to ignorant people with amateurish inquisitiveness was apparent. He was some-one who had his eye on faraway places and moved along the fringes of chaos and commotion, and he had only a few select companions. In a moment that was never repeated, tired and worn-out, in a sorrowful tone he spoke of that murky past to his confidant. "We were caught off guard, at our own hands. But that was not me. Not me before and not me after. What a letter of confession and repentance! What a hypocritical act I committed so that I would be released." And Mr. Far-vaneh's place in history remained unknown to all.

People generally knew him as the man he had been in recent years and as he appeared at building or neighborhood meetings: always well dressed, well groomed, and leaning on his cane, as if headed for a grand ceremony being held in his honor. With that rare self-confidence that doubtless was the fruit of mystical learnings and observations, he left an enduring impression on everyone. So much so that his statements about the harms of that animal odor once led the building residents to complain to City Hall by means of a neighborhood petition and a letter of grievance. "If, for example, the offspring of man and the cub of a wolf mature together in an enclosed space and under similar conditions, which do you think will adopt the other's characteristics? Therein lies your error." According to Mr. Farvaneh's research, it is man who will lose his identity, because animal instincts are so unyielding and strong that they will never be influenced by the behavior of any other species. "Yes, man became man when he withdrew from the animal kingdom; he distanced himself." Here, Mr. Farvaneh raised his index finger for emphasis. "And it is not without reason that this odor has surrounded us. It is conveying their invitation. It is an agent sent to reestablish contact."

Meanwhile, a few incidents strengthened Mr. Farvaneh's hypotheses. First was the animosity that developed between the residents of apartment thirteen and apartment nine. The feud seemed to be rooted in the positioning of cars in the building's garage, and sadly, sometime later, a verbal altercation led to a violent physical encounter between the gentlemen of the two apartments—an irrational conflict that ended in bloodshed. That day, Mr. Farvaneh didn't stay to witness the conclusion of the confrontation. Instead, he shook his head and proclaimed, "The gap has been closed." And he went up to his apartment and closed the door. A few minutes later, the scent of incense flowed onto the staircase and there was a bloody knife in the hands of a man who was crying.

"We must take action, if only for the sake of defending our humanity." Of course, no one paid much attention to Mr. Farvaneh's declaration. The health of the assailed, who was in the hospital, and the legal uncertainty surrounding the assailant were topics that deserved hours of heated discussion. It was for this same reason that the incident at the zoo didn't receive much attention, either, even though the death of two monkeys is a disaster for any zoo. The other monkeys mourned their dead with heartrending wails from dusk until dawn. There was also the sound of flapping wings and at times screams that rose from the throat of an unidentified animal. The following morning, the weather was exceptionally sunny, and Mr. Farvaneh spread the news of the monkeys' death.

"They are two fewer. This in itself is a divine gift. Two male monkeys have croaked. . . . Perhaps it would have been better if they had been females, but an eye for an eye." Then the old man was nowhere to be seen for several days. A month later, another noteworthy incident took place. One of the monkeys escaped from the zoo. The guards searched the nearby streets and buildings. Most excited and perhaps most terrified of all was Mr. Farvaneh, who kept pace with the guards and with a great degree of initiative followed the investigation. No one could convince him that the escaped monkey was not a serious threat. Well, if it were the lion or one of the wolves, then fine, but a small monkey? Regardless, Mr. Farvaneh took immediate action and installed steel bars on all his windows and his front door, and only after testing their sturdiness did he calm down a bit. Three days later, the escaped monkey was captured, and its arrest resulted in a letter of commendation for Mr. Farvaneh from the zoo's management.

It so happened that on that third day Mr. Farvaneh identified some sort of animal excrement on the building's stairs. This clue, and a trail of animal urine, together with Mr. Farvaneh's astuteness, led the guards to the rooftop and to an unused air-conditioning duct. What the monkey was doing out on the stairs in the middle of the night did not pique anyone's curiosity. Mr. Farvaneh, with a slight hint of satisfaction in his voice, said, "With their feces they mark their territory, imitating man's delineation of borders." And he drew a circle in the air and continued: "It is remarkable that if a man escapes from his cell, his sentence will become harsher, but this animal will receive no punishment at all because it has immunity. Beware, this time it was a monkey, but who knows." Then he raised his voice. "How can you be so sure that next time it won't be that python? Do you realize that each one of your children could be just a mouthful for it?" With this warning, he again encouraged the building's residents to prepare a neighborhood petition, but the experience of their previous failed attempt stopped them from taking any action. Their last effort was cut short in its final stage, which, in fact, was to obtain Mr. Farvaneh's signature. Before angrily dismissing the person collecting signatures, the old man had said, "Please remember, Farvaneh will never put his name on any document, especially collective ones." And the sound of the door slamming shut had shaken the entire building. Mr. Farvaneh's refusal to sign the petition was interpreted in two ways. Those who always dealt with the old man with a bit of humor attributed it to fear, and others concluded that he found it beneath him to put his signature on such a letter.

The residents soon forgot the incident with the monkey, as they did all of the others. But Mr. Farvaneh was not one to forget. For quite some time he was busy with the issues surrounding the monkey's escape, and finally, with deductions that were deemed beyond our comprehension and that forever remained in his heart, he grew silent. Naturally, one night the unused duct was secretly sealed.

Then came the winter of 1980—as gloomy and as cold as it was supposed to be, and so quiet and crawling that all its weeks can be summarized as one partly cloudy dawn and one rainy dusk. The bored bears in the zoo growled in their cement pits and the howls of the wolves grew more pained. But unlike all the other animals that huddled in the corner of their cages and pits and stared out with blank looks, the old rhinoceros, like a stone statue, would not leave the center of his pen. Did he like the rain? Did he understand something from it? By the way, no one can claim to have ever heard his sound or to be able to recognize it. Mr. Farvaneh said, "There are special rifles for hunting elephants and rhinoceroses. One bullet does the job. The animal's knees buckle and with no further effort it falls prostrate in front of the hunter. I have seen it in a film, and I think their falling to their knees so quickly should be the subject of works of art. Our stubborn rhinoceros, too, is standing in the center of his pen, waiting for just such a moment."

Whatever that animal's notion of death may have been, it had nothing to do with Mr. Farvaneh's regular Thursday evenings. The old man, looking most elegant in a dark suit and wearing a tie—which since the revolution has been considered "the leash of civilization" and is unofficially banned—would leave his apartment in the afternoon, buy a bouquet of flowers from his regular florist, and go visit his wife's grave. This was a routine he had picked up only in recent years. It seemed as if affection for this deceased, who remained forever patient despite her spouse's ill humor, had again blossomed in his heart. If at one time the grave of Mr. Farvaneh's wife had been in a quiet corner of the city's new cemetery, now the graves of those killed during the revolution and in the political unrest that followed had crowded the area. And so, unlike his wife, who was no longer alone, Mr. Farvaneh would return home sad and lonely. With grave stateliness, he would climb the stairs and insert the key in the lock on the steel gate and then unlock the apartment door and enter. A few minutes later, the smell of incense would swell on the landing, and it seemed as if from somewhere far away, from behind this wall and other walls, one could hear the sound of someone crying.

The first snow of that winter coincided with the death of another animal at the zoo. In the morning, a young lioness that was apparently born at the zoo was found in the middle of her cage with her claws brandished and reaching up to the sky, and thus the reason for the midnight roars that had robbed the neighborhood of sleep was revealed. In the days that followed, Mr. Farvaneh's provocations were quite a sight. "If you didn't know, then know now that it's been years since the race of lions has grown extinct in Iran, and these few that have taken refuge in this zoo do nothing other than inflict nightmares of themselves on our dreams. If only for a few minutes, imagine yourself buried up to your waist in the ground. Then, from among the shadows of the trees, one of them charges toward you. You want to sink in deeper, but you can't; you want to climb out and you can't, and he roars as he approaches you. Who will hear your pleas? Then he rubs his nose against your face and the smell of his breath . . . After the extinction of lions, one entire generation of humans has to come and go before having nightmares of them also grows extinct." It is likely that with his binoculars Mr. Farvaneh watched the frightful ceremony of the lioness's removal from her cage and from the side of her mate. "Of course, the best thing to do is to stuff their skin with hay and to put it on display in museums. This is a return to an ancient and forgotten tradition. By the way, what reason could there really be for the existence of deer without the lions?" Some people objected to Mr. Farvaneh's comments, stating that he should not say such things, that deer are beautiful animals. Mr. Farvaneh said, "Ugliness is repetitive beauty. These animals have been repeating themselves for thousands of years. It's enough."

Winter, too, was a season that had to pass. Other snow would fall, and every now and then watching it from the narrow corner of the window stirred in us a pleasant feeling of peace, the peace of descent. The dark snowflakes were indifferent to the geometric bodies of matter they fell onto. A sigh rose from within, fog formed on the window, and one was tempted to draw an image or to write something on it. Snow settled on the ground and people passed by. And the residents of the apartment building were indifferent to all of this, unless occasionally a learned man like Mr. Farvaneh took one of them by the hand and brought him to his apartment. He would pull the curtains aside and point to the footprints on the snow in front of the animal cages and say, "Look. What could the meaning of this upended principle be? The animal is sitting there staring at the trail of human footprints. Isn't it terrifying?" And then with trembling hands he would close the curtains before the baffled eyes of that person and collapse in the armchair. He would refuse to take any kind of sedative and rejected the offer of a glass of cold water. He would just hold his head in his hands and forget that someone else was present. But just as his anxious and uneasy guest would try to leave, Mr. Farvaneh would suddenly start to speak and ask him to stay for a while, for a few hours, in that living room, with the entire library at his disposal, even the armchair and the hunting binoculars. And then, trusting that someone was awake, he would try to sleep. He would leave his bedroom door ajar, and before sleep stole him away, he would jolt up several times to see if the aforementioned was still there or not. Perhaps the scene suggests some sort of old-age hallucination, but it wasn't. It was far more serious, because it was repeated time and again and in the exact same manner, and because in review-ing each instance, one sensed a singular cause, and that cause remained unknown to everyone. And apparently it had nothing to do with the death of seven or eight fla-mingos or the subsequent strange illness of a few deer. Although, after these incidents, Mr. Farvaneh's dis-temper did become more severe and fewer people were willing to spend a few hours in his living room so that he could sleep. Everyone made an excuse. Everyone had an excuse, and spring, needing no excuse, arrived.

Mr. Farvaneh said, "Let's assume it isn't so. But you haven't paid attention. I can prove it." Then he led his listener to his apartment, unlocked the steel gate and the front door, and walked straight to the window overlooking the zoo. He nervously pulled the curtains aside and said, "Look. Here are the binoculars. Their mating is not animalistic. They don't show the same characteristics as they do in the forest or the desert.

Before onlookers, like a spectacle. Perhaps it's an expert imitation of human intercourse. No, it's far too much of a mockery. Pay attention!" He handed over the binoculars and retreated to the armchair, and finally, as if it were the first time he had made this request, he said, "I beseech you not to leave. In my library there are precious collections on any subject that might interest you. I will lock the front door because you may not notice something entering while you are immersed in a book. But I will leave the bedroom door ajar." Fully dressed and exhausted from severe insomnia, he fell on the bed, and, just as previous times, before falling asleep, he looked several times to make sure the other person was still there, and then a sleep akin to death, with no dreams or nightmares, embraced him.

Those who had this experience, which in the rumor mill was referred to as "babysitting," would not fall into the same trap twice. When they ran into Mr. Farvaneh, if they were compelled to stop and listen to him, they refrained from any expressions of doubt or disagreement. Rapid movements of the head as a sign of agreement were followed by a hasty excuse that they offered while climbing or descending the stairs, and this ended the encounter before Mr. Farvaneh could finish his comments.

In a voice void of enthusiasm, Mr. Farvaneh said, "The turning point in any creature's life is the moment it is caught off guard. Don't worry, you won't be caught off guard, because you have been caught before. Some creatures, I mean many, are only afflicted once. Like the elephant that asserts his victory over man by not breaking his chains. I have not been defeated; on the contrary, once again I face being caught off guard, and there's nothing I can do. There was nothing I could do to begin with. Look here, five or six years ago, in a completely protected lair, a wolf was born, one meant specifically for the zoo, and it was reared for this exact purpose. Instead of teaching him hunting techniques, his mother taught him how to find the traps set by the hunters under contract to the zoo. That wolf is now here, and coincidence has had no hand in its fate. And I say—please pay attention—I say, because I spend more time watching and watch more carefully, and because I am aware of their collective thoughts, I am a target. Yes, this is the right word, target. I said . . . I mean . . . I'm sorry, you don't seem to be listening."

Spring, too, came and went. When summer arrived, for several weeks I didn't see Mr. Farvaneh. I was traveling, and I don't know whether my conscience should bear the burden of guilt for this negligence or not. However, when I returned, nothing was said to me for an entire week—surely not because the event lacked importance. Perhaps the neighbors were all under the impression that I knew. I don't know how sometimes some words are left unspoken, with no collusion but with some sort of a tacit agreement and with that particular cruelty of mankind. In any case, no one told me Mr. Farvaneh had died until I myself inquired about his health after having repeatedly faced the unanswered door of his apartment. I don't claim any sort of affection between myself and that honorable man. In mourning him, I did not suffer that grief we experience after the death of relations or loved ones. More than anything, I was driven to think, and I cannot say how or why. I don't intend to express surprise, not from the fact that the bookseller had seen Mr. Farvaneh leaving the zoo on several occasions despite his repugnance of the place, and not even from the concurrence of these visits with the deaths of animals. Incidents such as the discovery of that monkey near the duct on the roof and the surprising silence of the zoo on the night Mr. Farvaneh died do not perplex me; they only intrigue the frivolous curiosity of idle minds, nothing more. But the sum of Mr. Farvaneh's statements, explicit and implicit, remains etched in my memory. What he actually meant to say, whether he succeeded or not, is obvious to me. But meanings, often, contrary to common perception, are the image of their own meaninglessness. Therefore, paying too much attention to them is pointless. But sometime after his death, in a manner that is not worthy of mention, I gained entry to the old man's apartment. I locked the steel gate and the front door behind me and in that dimly lit, archaic place I suddenly found myself isolated and excluded. The scent of incense still lingered in corners, and the bed in which the old man's heart had stopped was still rumpled and remindful of the violent convulsions of death. The source of my sorrow was mostly the question of whether it was truly necessary for several days to go by before the others

learned of Farvaneh's death from the stench of putre-
faction that had overpowered the smell of the zoo.

Was the old man really found in a state suggest-
ing that he had suffered some terrible horror? Were
his arms braced in front of him and were his eyes wide
with the realization of his nightmare? I didn't touch
the heavy curtains. For a while I stood there staring at
the armchair and the old lamp next to it, and as I left
that apartment, I wasn't as surprised at seeing that the
lenses of his hunting binoculars were broken as I was at
finding empty the shelf that held his collection of books
on animal lives.

Mummy and Honey

D URING THE SEVENTH-DAY OBSERVANCE of Grand-father's passing, paying no heed to the comings and goings of those serving tea and sweet drinks in the five-windowed drawing room, with its gilded scales glistening, it gently coiled around the bitter orange tree and disappeared among its branches and leaves. No one saw it but the youngest brother, who had that day arrived from abroad. With eyes that from sleeplessness and a thousand thoughts had turned poppy red, he clumsily suffered through the ceremony, now and then turning to stare out at the bitter orange tree, hoping to see again the glittering reflection of the viper. And he didn't.

In the evening, when the house emptied of outsiders, Father summoned all three brothers to Grandfather's room. He had already moved his belongings there. He would sleep on Grandfather's carved-wood bed and from that man's easy chair he would issue household orders. He spoke with conviction and fatigue. From that day on, all three brothers were to take up residence in that ancestral home, or their monthly allowance would be cut off. Grandfather, to compensate for his absence in that dwelling, and so that the remaining members of the dispersed dynasty would come together again, had so willed. And he, their father, to preserve the dying tradition of their ancestors, so desired. The youngest brother raised his voice. He flailed his delicate arms and shouted that he had not completed his studies abroad, and besides, he said, lowering his voice, he might have plans to marry a suitable, like-minded girl. But Father, seated on that easy chair, waved his hand, as if gently pushing something away, closed his eyes, and went to sleep. Stunned, the three brothers descended the stone staircase. In the cavernous kitchen, half-burned logs sputtered in wood-burning stoves. The eldest brother said they must obey and went to his quarters.

The house was sprawling. The courtyard was surrounded by the two-story structure, and on each side, rooms with five full-length windows faced the large jasper green pool at its center. Father had assigned each of them a separate wing. In their rooms, the brothers stared at the wooden beams in the ceiling until dawn and listened to the rustle that crept above them. . . . The next day, the eldest brother moved his wife and belongings to the house, but the other brothers' quarrel with Father continued. Father would shout, "What is there left of us? . . . The Zand dynasty is scattered. You took wives from breeds with new money. . . . What about blood, lineage, pedigree? . . . From whom will your children learn our ways? . . . You indolent loafers, leave if you can. I will not give an allowance to anyone who doesn't honor the spirit of his father's forebearers. . . ."

Out of earshot, the youngest brother mumbled, "He's lost his mind. Opium and the death of that one-hundred-and-thirty-year-old who fed on ill-gotten gains have dried up his brain. I'll bring him to his senses, you'll see. . . ." But the middle brother seemed to have been persuaded, and hoping for a temporary stay, he yielded to Father's old-age whims and a week later transferred his wife and belongings from the apartment he rented in the northern part of town to the house. The following night, the sound of his hammered dulcimer and his wife's singing rang from their five-windowed drawing room. His wife was a seductress with an added veil of flesh across the curves of her body. She was one of those women with whom few men could practice restraint and endurance. Late into their nights of lovemaking, her lustful groans would penetrate even the farthest corners of the house. Father would shout, "Enough . . . enough!" But the sound of the woman's sweat-drenched, vindictive laughter would spiral around his room. And when daylight came, the woman would occupy the courtyard more brazenly than the day before. The eyes of the stained-glass windows would darken before her mercilessly voluptuous and commanding gait, and at the sound of her raspy voice, hundreds of sparrows would take flight from along the narrow watercourse that circled the pool.

It was she who saw the viper the second time. She ran shrieking into the courtyard. She had seen a rope in the middle of her room, and when she bent down to pick it up, the rope had with insolent reluctance slithered into the folds of the bedding. Father said, "She's lying. She's acting up." The middle brother, while consoling his wife, replied, "Why in the world do we have to live here? You're being stubborn. Why can't we all move to a new house? We can buy an apartment building and each take a separate floor." Father scoffed, "Even if there is a snake, what is it doing inside a room when there's the roof and the baby pigeons, the bitter oranges and the sparrows? . . ." And he bent over the brazier and opium smoke wafted into the air.

The youngest brother brought Father's double-barreled shotgun from the storeroom and loaded it. Mumbling something about a university degree tossed to the wind and a fair-figured lover with eyes like the ocean cast to the sea, he sat in ambush under the bitter orange tree in which he had first seen that golden shimmer. The bitter orange trees were great in number. They were planted in a tight row around the twenty-three-foot-long pool of unknown depth, and the aged green of their leaves blended with the algaed water. The youngest brother growled, "This entire mausoleum is a maze. Where am I going to find that creature?" And he immediately grew quiet and listened.

Near dusk, the sparrows suddenly flew off in fright from a tree nearby, and he ran and aimed the shotgun at the dense leaves, which in the fading light of early evening were no longer green. A bloated, rotting bitter orange left over from the previous year fell to the ground and he fired. Dust rose in the air and petals fell from the blossoms, but no viper came into view.

And then Father walked down the stone stairs, rinsed his hands in the pool, and said, "I'm telling you . . . leave that snake alone. If it develops a grudge against you, it will even cross the ocean to hunt you down." The youngest brother moaned, "But why, Father? I promise to return when I finish my studies. I owe only a small sum over there. . . . Support me for one more year. . . . Why do you insist that I rot in these cellars and storerooms? I'll die here." Father pointed to the weeds growing on the clay and straw rooftops and said, "You're dead already. . . . Look . . . listen!" In the pallor of the last light of day, unearthly gossamer waves with a faint trace of vermilion floated above the walls and across the dark windows of the second floor, and the black swifts darted about amid their folds. Father said, "They observe our actions, ready and alert. . . . The moment you turn your back to them, you're dead. . . . Why don't you come sit beside me and savor a smoke? . . ." The son, disgusted and crippled by hatred, escaped to his room and closed the door.

In the days that followed, although the fear of a viper that could be anywhere swelled in the seven cavities of their bodies, they were more preoccupied with discovering a means of escape from an oppressive eternity in that house. And all this time, the eldest son's wife was silent. Every afternoon she would sit on the stone edge of the pool and stare at the murky water with her doelike eyes, which bore the gravity of an unspeakable secret and the gleam of determination. In the early hours of dusk, when the water no longer mirrored the sun's radiance, in it one could detect the ghostly passage of large algae-encrusted fish. Small worms, red and pearly-colored, would swim up and cling to the surface for an instant and then, with amusing twists and turns, they would again sink.

Occasionally, the late-afternoon breeze would coat the water with bitter orange blossoms. The layer of petals would ripple and the watchful woman would imagine a snake floating beneath it. The next day, the sodden clusters of translucent petals would sink into the water and one could again see the shadowy trace of the old fish.

Doe Eyes placed bowls of salted water all around the house. "Snakes like it. The snake will drink it, and when it does, it will feel beholden to us and won't try to hurt us." One early morning, she jolted awake with her eyes wide and, moved by the dream she had had, she said, "Blood will be shed in this house. . . . I am certain of it. . . . Dreams that come to me in the early hours of the morning always come true."

After the fortieth-day ceremony of Grandfather's passing, no kin set foot in that house again. Father was convinced that everyone was lying in wait to somehow plunder his inheritance. His calculated ill temper had driven them all away. And in return, relatives resolved to drive his sons away. They were left with only an old half-breed albino who, together with his mute wife, maintained the house and cooked.

Father liked all of them to gather together for meals. The women, with the help of the mute hag, would bring in the food and the faience plates on ornate copper trays and they would all sit around the dinner cloth spread on the carpet and eat without looking at one another. One day, the youngest brother kicked his plate aside and growled, "If I am to die in this damn house, then I won't eat another bite for it to be over sooner. . . ." And he got up and walked out. Father, unperturbed, crawled on all fours over to where his son had been sitting and carefully gathered the rice that had spilled from his plate. "He'll come begging when he gets hungry." The middle brother's wife burst into tears and covered her face with her hands.

That afternoon, in response to an attempt at mediation by the eldest brother, Father's shouts reverberated all through the house. "You, shut up! . . . What is their right and rightful share? . . . They have no share. . . ." The eldest brother, with his shoulders slouched, descended the stone stairs. The courtyard was flooded with the scent of bitter orange blossoms, and the black swifts glided above it in all directions. Then everyone, even the youngest brother, who was up on the roof, lying in wait for the viper, heard the sound of Father's sobs.

The middle brother beat the delicate hammers on the dulcimer strings. His wife threw open all five windows of their drawing room and the instrument's centuries-old echo of secrets and murmur of malice silenced the swallows and sparrows. The old half-breed and his wife came up from the kitchen and sat in the courtyard, leaning against the stone reliefs that skirted the walls of the house, and gazed at the open windows of the drawing room. The doe-eyed woman turned her eyes away from the pool. Then the brazen minx appeared in the frame of the first window and, with a sly smile on her face, unleashed a dance that was shorn of dancing. She leaned back, and in concert with her swaying arms, the quiver of her proud breasts poured across the courtyard. Amid the gleams of light floating in the air, there was a slith-ering streak. It twirled and emerged in the frame of the second window. The beat of the music grew faintly more rapid. The youngest brother shouted from the rooftop. The woman's arms reached up, coiled around each other like two snakes, and the scent of a carefree spirit mingled with the perfume of blossoms. The woman puckered her lips, raised her eyebrows, and winked at the dark, closed windows of the other three wings of the house. She swayed her body, stomped her feet, and the jingle of invisible ankle bracelets reverberated among the branches and leaves. The woman was in the third window and the tempo of the music increased. . . . A mysterious smile spread across Doe Eye's lips, and the half-breed albino bared his festering, toothless gums in silent laughter. The dulcimer strings trembled. In the fourth window, the minx's unearthly limbs, writhing and restless, swung to all sides. The bitter orange blossoms rained on the pool. The woman ululated. Her drenched hair spilled onto her shoulders and its curls sprang open with stinging leaps. Loud and venomous, the sound of the dulcimer echoed in the rooms and antechambers and seeped out from the structure's countless pores. A few strings snapped and lay crimped at the edge of the instrument, and the man still struck the blistering hammers. . . . The fifth window was wrapped in dusk, and the specter of the woman's venge-ful figure undulated in the dark. . . . In the end, she cried out and fell in a swoon.

All this time, Father's shadow lingered behind the green, garnet, and agate stained-glass windows of his room. That night, their customary dinner spread was not laid out. The others took shelter in the darkness of their respective wings and listened to the minx's rapturous gasps, which were more blatant than ever before. But at midnight, except for the youngest brother, who remained on the rooftop in a gale of moonlight and noxious stars, no one heard Father's painful cry. "G . . . Go . . . God . . . why are they doing this to me?"

Two days passed with the fevered hallucinations of the starving youngest brother. Armed with the shotgun, he searched every crook and corner of the house, looking for the viper. He pushed aside ghosts that crossed his path with a curse and one by one he swung open the doors and advanced. The eldest brother drew in the opium smoke, lay down, and stared at the ceiling crowded with bright red phantasms that rippled into one another. The minx sat by the pool, dipped her feet in the water, and, in response to the sparrows' chirping, smiled cunningly, aware of Father's eyes behind the windows of his room.

On the third day, they had just sat down to lunch when the youngest brother's delirious shouts rang out from the cellars. The middle brother cautiously said, "He will die of hunger. . . ." Father sneered, "No one in our dynasty has ever died of hunger. . . . He won't, either." Then he turned to the women and in a conciliatory tone asked, "Why aren't you bearing children? My father hoped to see his grandchildren and great-grandchildren in this house. And I want to see his great-great-grandchild." Doe Eyes blushed and looked down. The eldest brother said, "Children are nothing but a headache. This house is crowded enough as it is. . . ." And he got up.

That afternoon, sitting by the pool, the minx saw a golden glow from the corner of her eyes. She turned and screamed. The youngest brother came running. He lowered the gun lock's catch and aimed, but he wavered. Before his fevered eyes, under the jasmine bushes, outstretched and wondrous, slithered cold conceit and spellbinding doom. The defeated man moaned. The woman stomped her feet and screamed in horror, "Kill it! . . . Kill it! . . ." The flickering gleam, visible and invisible, was moving toward a cellar stocked with firewood. The woman beat her fists on the dazed man's shoulders. "Kill it! . . . Kill it! . . ." The trigger was pulled. Slugs shattered against the flax-colored Cossack bricks bordering the flower patch and dust rose in the air. The woman howled and the man fired again. Lead pellets ricocheted off the bricks. The viper turned to face them. "Kill it! . . . Kill it! . . ." The youngest brother clumsily reloaded the shotgun, but he didn't have time to shoot. All he could do was move the woman and himself out of the way of that golden gleam that sprang at them. Behind them, the hiss from an ungratified jaw moved away. Father shouted, "Idiots! . . . You fools! . . . You've wounded it. Who in the world kills a house snake? He will not let you off. . . . He'll kill you." The minx leaned her forehead against the wall and burst into tears. The youngest brother dropped the shotgun and looking dazed; he went toward the vestibule. "I will leave this place. . . . I will leave and never come back. . . ."

The eldest brother grumbled. The middle brother took his anger out on the bushes on that side of the courtyard, pulling them all out by the roots, but there was no sign of the viper. The eldest brother said, "The earth is under the rule of the snake. If the snake wants, the earth will open up and hide it." Nights and days fraught with fear lay ahead of them. With each step they took, they anticipated a vengeful bite. The arabesque motif on the carpet suddenly appeared to be a snake. Under the chests, there was enough space for a helix lying in wait. Each time they walked into a room, they rediscovered their own wretched ankles and calves. Cabinet doors were shut tight on an infinite darkness, somewhere in which glistened a pair of crimson crystals.

The minx never set foot in the garden again and the nights in her five-windowed drawing room grew silent and bleak. In the middle of the night, she would wake up screaming from the touch of something cold. She would cower on top of the ice chest, and while vomiting her horror, she would make her husband search their bedding and every corner of the room. Doe Eyes increased the number of saltwater bowls. They called a snake catcher, a grimy-looking man with cold, steady eyes. When he saw the house, he said it would be difficult to find a snake in that sprawling compound; he had to move in for a few days. He started with the rooftops and made his way down to the courtyard. Wherever he found a hole, he would blow snake-charming breaths and incantations into it, and a short distance away he would squat down and stare at it. Father watched his actions with contempt and said, "I told you . . . I told you to leave that poor thing alone." The snake catcher replied, "There's opium smoke in this house. The snake is probably hooked. There's no way it will leave." And he went on smearing his yellowed saliva around gaps and along cracks, until one morning they found his darkened corpse in one of the cellars. There were fang marks on his jugular, blood and dark foam had oozed from the corner of his mouth, and there was a white snake's egg in his fist.

Father laughed out loud, the eldest brother increased his daily dose of opium, and the minx started to speak again. She paced up and down the five-windowed room and repeated over and over again, "Go away . . . go away. . . ." When she grew tired, she sat, but she would quickly jump up again in a panic and look around. Occasionally, they heard terrified shrieks from the sparrows' nests under the eaves. Panic-stricken birds would fly into the air and everyone would know that the viper was devouring their chicks. The middle brother, when he wasn't carrying a stick and searching the house, scoured the streets in search of the youngest brother and took measure of the cold and unkind conduct of their relatives. Discouraged, he would return home, only to face his wife's distraught laments. "Why did you leave me alone in this viper's nest?"

One day, the half-breed albino said he had seen the snake with its head in the stew pot. The minx cried, "It wants to torture us to death! That creature is intelligent. . . ." She pointed to Father's drawing room. "He will kill us all! He wants us to spew blood, turn blue, and die." Then with her eyes wide, she suddenly grew silent and listened. There was a rustle in the ceiling, in the walls, too; golden scales floated in the air. . . . "It wants me. It wants to bite me before it bites the rest of you. . . ." And she clung to her husband's legs. "Let's leave this place. . . . Let's go away. . . ." The man gnawed at his mustache and, burning with blind hatred, growled, "With what money? Have patience. I'll burn this house to the ground. I'll send that snake and its venom up in smoke. . . ."

They sometimes saw tufts of feathers, pluckings from the massacre of sparrow chicks, fall from the eaves. And just then, on the other side of the courtyard, at the foot of the spear-wielding stone soldiers of the wall reliefs, a stream of molten gold would sink into the log-filled cellar. They slept with the lights on. One night, the minx opened her eyes and saw a half ray of sun on the ceiling. The woman lay still and surrendered to the horror. Right above her, the viper was hanging from a wooden beam, staring at her with dead eyes. Staring into the snake's steady gaze, she felt a crippling cold spread from her neck down to her limbs. Her hands went numb, then her middle and her legs. Scale by scale, the chill of death spread across her. She opened her mouth and, in the same voice that she used to beckon her mate on carousing nights, whispered, "Come to me . . . come. . . ." In the morning, she had no recollection of how many hours she had lain motionless beneath that cold blade, staring up at the viper's jaw open in an eternal sneer. In the doorway of the vestibule, the middle brother took the woman's hands and begged, "Don't go. . . ." The woman's eyes were sunken, her white crystalline skin had turned haggishly sallow and dehydrated, and she kept flicking her tongue over her lips like a snake. She said nothing, and dragging her small suitcase behind her, she sank into the darkness of the vestibule.

The house took on the quiet that Father had decreed. The old man laid his hand on the middle brother's shoulder and said, "That harlot wasn't good enough for you. All the better that she left. . . ." On the now blossomless bitter orange trees, young green fruit were plumping. Once in a while, one would fall onto the Cossack bricks with a muted thud and it would bounce and roll away like a ball. Early evenings, the defeated sound of the middle brother's dulcimer could be heard from behind the five closed windows of his drawing room. Doe Eyes would sit by the pool, stare into the gaping mouth of a stone lion, and gently run her fingers through the water. A little farther away, the half-white, half-black old man would splash water around the courtyard with a copper watering can and the bricks would sizzle, a mist would rise, and the intoxicating dust would blend into a fog with the dulcimer's ancient sobs and the woman's dark gaze on the water.

Father resumed allowance payments to the two older brothers. He showed that he could be magnanimous. "Go buy whatever you want for yourselves. . . . There's enough to last us seven generations."

But the ever-present ghosts were not gratified for long. After noontime prayers, lunch had been laid out and they were wallowing in the perfume of rice and tallow when the youngest brother walked in. Disheveled and ragged, he sat down, tucked the baby rabbit he was holding in the crook of his knee, and, without uttering a word, pulled the platter of rice toward him and began wolfing down the food as if he had not eaten in all that time. Father watched him with a gentle and forgiving smile. "You see . . . in the end we all come back here." That afternoon, the youngest brother snapped the rabbit's neck and left it at the foot of a bitter orange tree. The next morning, there was no sign of the dead animal. "This was a peace offering. . . . If we feed it, it will probably forgive us and leave us alone. . . . May the spirit of our great ancestor bless us. . . . Amen."

In the days that followed, with the shotgun in his hand and a mysterious glint in his eyes, the youngest brother sat in ambush in a corner of the courtyard, and as soon as a flock of sparrows gathered along the water-course that circled the pool, he would shoot. The commotion of wounded chirps and fluttering wings would rise and he would run and snap off the sparrows' heads, leaving their carcasses here and there around the house. Doe Eyes secretly wept for the sacrificed, and, terrified of the scheme that was brewing in whispers between the younger brothers in the alcoves and recesses of the house, she prayed to the prophets for help. The youngest brother said, "The day will come when we give this side of the house to the viper. We have fed and fattened it. It will settle in the drawing room. We will no longer fear it and it will no longer spite us. We will confide in it; we will celebrate with it, sleep beside it. An old twenty-two-foot-long viper . . ."

With the weather warming, they spread carpets over wooden platform beds they had set up by the pool and they ate dinner there in the shelter of the bitter orange trees. The gillyflowers had bloomed by the hundreds and the timeless house was filled with their fragrance. Father, delighting in the coming together of the family, would reminisce about Grandfather, his forebearers, lands and estates, old conflicts and feuds. "This peace and comfort is the fruit of the battles and braveries of the men of our dynasty. Be grateful and honor them. We are of them and live for them." Then everyone would grow silent and listen to the breeze waft through the bitter orange trees. . . .

At midnight, when the house became the realm of ghosts Father conjured, the youngest brother would go to the rooms of the middle brother and they would talk in the dark until the early hours of the morning. And one afternoon when the residents of the house became certain that the viper was not alone, the two brothers showed no surprise. Undaunted and with a confidence rooted in their subconscious minds, they watched the viper's consort. On the bed beside the pool, the two were engaged in a mating dance. An inaudible tune tempered their movements. They brought their heads together, withdrew, and, close to one another, half rose and craned

back and forth to the left and right of each other. Father
let out a spirited laugh and said, "They will bear children.
. . . It's a good omen. A snake is a harbinger of good. Its
spine brings sympathy; its brood brings bounty. . . ." And
together with the eldest brother, they took to the brazier
and smoked more than ever before. The youngest brother
whispered to the middle brother, "It's time. . . ."

That night, having made certain that everyone was
asleep, the two walked out into the courtyard. The
flickering glow of the kerosene lamp in Father's room
stretched as far as the pool. Barefoot, the two climbed
the stone stairs up to his room. The youngest brother
had said, "Just a few drops . . . He sleeps so soundly
when he is high and delirious, it's as if he's dead. . . .
We'll put only a few drops in his ear. . . . He'll sleep
forever. . . . May God forgive the dead. . . ." The middle brother quietly opened the door. Like ghosts, they
crept in. Father, heavy and regal, was sleeping at the far
end of the room, his steady breaths the essence of time.
The two brothers took a step forward but then froze in
place. At the foot of Father's bed, a pair of vipers raised
their heads from their coil the instant they sensed the
warmth of the brothers' presence. They opened their
jaws and hissed. The brothers, with deadened hearts
and drenched in bitter sweat, forever retreated. . . .

Many long years remained until Father's 110th
year, and the day of his passing, when they would
unseal his last will and testament to learn that with the
same stipulation as Grandfather's, their inheritance had
been entrusted to the eldest brother.

Shatter the Stone Tooth

HE WROTE OF THE UNTIMELY HEAT IN GURAAB, of its sun that seems to shine a blinding purple, of a cavern with forty-four stairs and an image carved on its wall. And he wrote of a dog that "transfers his fantasies of smell and sound to his companion." All of which I don't understand. He wrote that he has a hut at the far end of the village, where at night he writes on the walls; he didn't say what. Probably those verses that men hum under their breath or scribble somewhere when they feel lonely. He wrote that he doesn't intend to come to town for the weekends anymore, that the days in Guraab are the end of time and it's best that he wait there. Then he wrote a lot about the mud huts that are connected to one another by underground tunnels, and of villagers with trachoma, and of "gusts of dust that get into your throat and make you retch," and he wrote, "Would you believe that dust can rot?" I can't believe he wrote this letter. His earlier letters were not like this; they were real letters. Even his handwriting used to enchant me. His letters were filled with words that men in love string together and that every woman loves to read or hear, even though just after they are read or heard they seem banal. But now look . . . lately . . . I will read so you can understand what I mean:

"When they all take it upon themselves to kill a living thing but it doesn't die and even goes so far as to trust them again, I realize that all the things I have ever said to you were just an illusion, the fantasies of a dog with seven lives who knows the secret to the image carved on the wall and whose fifth life is about to end."

In the days when he used to come to town, it was autumn and winter. We would go for a stroll on a quiet street. Perhaps you did this sort of thing, too, when you were engaged. Not much of it stays in one's memory, not the words that were spoken, not the jokes, perhaps only the image of feet treading in unison and the memory of a tree-lined dead-end alley that didn't look like a dead end. And one more memory—the smell of wintersweet flowers floating from behind the walls of a house on a rainy day. In those days, if I asked him to talk about the place where he was stationed, he would say, "Let's not talk about it." Maybe he just didn't want to change the subject. Then he would carefully look around to see if we were alone, and he would take my hand or he would . . . And he wrote nothing about Guraab. Perhaps he thought I would worry if I knew where he was stuck and how he was suffering. But he was becoming so unsettled. I could sense there was something wrong.

Then, after two months of not having sent any news of himself, a letter arrived in May. The one that is mostly about Guraab. He wrote that there are some words that cannot be carved on the wall or spoken to anyone; they can only be written in a letter, so that while writing them one can picture their effect on the reader's face. At the end he wrote two or three lines about that dog, and good-bye. With no "I hope to see you soon," or "I kiss your eyes," or even tell me to say hello to this or that person. Do you know what he used to write in the early days? "My soul mate . . ." and other words that I cannot repeat. I would write back, "You careless boy, what if they open your letter at the post office, what then . . . what would they think?" It was obvious that he was painfully lonely, but whatever it was, his thoughts were with me and the time when his military service would end. Now you tell me what this means:

"At noon, I walk down the stairs of the cavern. I take a lantern with me; it's hell outside. A greasy sweat seeps from my pores; I thirst for water, but I vomit the minute I drink. The men of Guraab, a few here and there, are sitting in the shadow of their huts, smoking water pipes; they whisper to one another and keep a watchful eye on the road. They're not concerned with me, and I'm comfortable down here where the vapors of the earth bloat and swell. I sit in the middle of the circular wall and listen. I hear sounds. Besides the steady sound of water trickling, there are voices that linger here from a thousand years ago or even before. Someone screamed, someone lit a fire, the condemned ones laughed, and others uttered incantations."

What anxiety his May letter caused me and, worse, the letters that followed. I wrote to him, "It's better if you don't talk about Guraab. No matter how cursed the place, you are there; you represent the Development Corps; you are there to help them.* Think of how important your work is from a humanitarian point of view." I couldn't string together complicated words like he could. In any case, I meant "I admire you for your service." Then, as though he had developed a grudge against me, too, he started sending these letters, some only a day apart. Like this one, only three lines—it's obvious he wrote it in a hurry. And what does it say? That they are lying in ambush, waiting to capture him and to strangle him with a rope, but they still don't know where he's hiding. He wrote that he alone knows of this hiding place and, of course, he won't tell them. Four times he repeated it: He won't tell them, won't tell them . . .

No. How could I go? There are times when I don't even dare walk alone in the streets of our own town. I dreamed that a few men were chasing me, in the middle of the day, and nobody paid any attention. I ran through the crowds, screaming. The men caught up with me. . . . Would my father go with me? Could I go alone? I wanted to. What he must have thought of me. . . . Besides, I was scared. I'm still scared of Guraab. If people there are anything like the way he describes them, they would have strung me up in the middle of the village square. What? Where did he write it? Read! Right here: "Forty or fifty huts made of sun-dried bricks

---

* Skilled and literate conscripts are sent to remote villages to promote development and to aid villagers with health, education, and modern agricultural techniques.

in the middle of a sunken plain, and on three sides of the plain, high mountains of sulfurous sandstone and slabs of slippery rock. No trees, no water. When soil rots, it sucks up the water and it seems as if it has never rained. The decay is spreading. It will scale up the pass and infest the surrounding plains and overrun everything." Well, isn't this frightening? He wrote:

"There's another village on this plain, it's called Gur-Gedaa, and guys from there come around here to steal. Dark-skinned, with even darker, dazed eyes. I'm frightened. I'm frightened of the look in their eyes. They, too, shun me, like all the others. Only this dog runs to me whenever he sees me. He comes and sniffs at my ankles. It's as if he smells a scent that I'm incapable of smelling myself. Even more appalling is the wheat crop. It has already turned yellow and it's pathetically sparse and short. I tell these godforsaken people, 'Why do you fool yourselves into thinking that you will have a good harvest this year?' Their joy and gratefulness make me even more nervous."

He had told some guy named Farvardin, "Why are you so resigned? If you go to town and work as a laborer, you will have a better life. There's water there for you to wash yourself. You'll have some money to check out the town in the evenings; you'll see colors, you can go to the movies, and you will see things you've never even dreamed of. If you go uptown, you'll see beauty and well-being all concentrated in one place, and you will finally realize that Sabz-Ali's sister isn't such a great catch after all."

He wrote: "No one here has ever seen the sea. They haven't even seen a river. Once in a while they see a flood and they climb up to the top of the hill, where the crevice leading to the cavern has split open. When the water subsides, they go back and rebuild their huts, a couple fewer each time. Just yesterday, someone sold his daughter. They plucked her eyebrows and made her up and sent her to an Arab on the other side of the Gulf. Maybe she won't even make it to the other side. The kid had her heart set on getting some candy. Her father, Sadegh, needed the money to take his wife to town to give birth. The woman is past her eleventh month and still hasn't given birth. The child is alive in her belly, but it will neither die nor come out. They say they can hear it cry. I went to the cavern to avoid hearing it. The dog had taken refuge there, too. He was sitting there, listening. I am amazed at what this animal finds to eat around here. There isn't enough to feed the humans. I share my food with him. Sometimes he disappears for a few days. Maybe he goes to Gur-Gedaa. . . ."

Obviously, it was a large dog. An animal that doesn't choke to death when they throw ropes around his neck and pull from both sides must be quite a beast. He wrote: "He's white, with black spots, and he's constantly panting from the heat. If spring isn't over yet and it's already this hot, the summer must be hell. I take off my clothes and try to sleep in the dark cavern." At the end of his letter, he asked me, in the middle of the night, when it's quiet everywhere, to go and turn on the water faucet so that water dripped from it. He wanted me to listen to the *drip, drip* sound in the dark. He wrote that the sound bears a secret and for those who discover it, all places in the world will become identical. Don't say it . . . no . . . you, of all people, don't say it. . . . Everyone tells me what's the use. . . . Don't tell me that, either. Let me cry and unburden myself. And don't tell me that I'm still young and that I should be thinking of my future and my happiness. I don't want to. I wrote to him, "Without you, I won't exist. Think of me, too. I don't even want a wedding. Just come back. Let's get married, have kids, and then go wherever you want and chase after whatever dream you have." I wrote that I'm still full of life. . . . I put all caution aside; I thought perhaps his feelings for me would be rekindled. I wrote, "Your life is still here. . . ."

No, he didn't come. He wrote he has realized that the existence of the carved image in the cavern is not without significance. A stone man was standing there. He wrote that he was cleaning the rest of the carving; then maybe he could understand what it meant . . . with the help of his companion, the dog. . . . When he was here, I never saw him avoid people. He was simple and quiet, but he certainly wasn't shy with me. He was spirited and exciting. I was sure that once he fell into the routine of life, he would really make something of himself. Any woman would have known that once he started to work, if his heart was content, he would provide a decent life for his family. And then this same man turned into such a recluse that he wrote he can no longer stand the light, that the sun shines to blind him.

He wrote: "Despite all their ignorance, the poor villagers sometimes play me for a fool in their own way, and I get it. I tell them, 'You poor slobs, leave, go somewhere else, migrate to the seaside. You have never seen a rice paddy; you don't know what it smells like. . . .'" They laughed at him. I'm sure they laughed at him when he said such things. They put him on the spot and asked, "Who are you? What do you do? Why don't you know anything?" They blamed him for a couple of their palm trees drying up. "Farvardin was shouting at me, asking me why the well has dried up. I don't know, I don't know why none of the wells reaches water. They keep killing their hens one after the other. It's a bad omen if hens cluck at dawn, and some of the hens have started clucking at dawn. Rostam says, 'What do you think . . . what is wrong with the hens? Why don't they want to sit on their eggs? . . . What do you think we should plant in this soil?' I don't know. Bibi Golabatun says, 'Then what did you come here for?' I tell her I don't know. She says, 'Our own men understand soil, seed, and rain better than you. These men have planted this land for generations and they'll be here to the very last day, not you.' I don't know what to say. I came here just to finish what's left of my service and go home."

He actually took a few of them by the hand and led them into the cavern to show them the image. It took him a month to clean away the centuries-old dirt and to reveal part of it. A wheat field—or something similar—was carved into the stone. The man's hand wasn't empty. He was holding a dagger. . . . I think he lost all hope and confidence in his work when he didn't manage to save the palm trees. He wrote: "Here, the sparse wheat grows only out of a thousand-year-old habit; it is only an illusion of the fertility that existed centuries ago. Once the wheat realizes that it's only an illusion, it stops growing." He wrote: "Rostam dragged me to his plot of land to boast about his harvest this year. I told him it's no good. He broke off a stalk and counted the seeds, thirteen of them. He said it's full. I said it's as little as alms for a beggar. He walked into the field, held his arms open wide, and hollered, 'Do you even know how I've struggled here, you who come from the big city?' I told him that whether I know or not, this soil is dead, it no longer breathes, and it can't be cured with fertilizers. He was insulted. He lunged at me. I turned my back to him and headed for the village, and he stood there clenching the thirteen seeds in his fist and yelling. Bibi Golabatun says I bring a curse to Guraab because the dog walks in my shadow. I told her, 'You are your own curse. If that dog peeks in through the door of your hut and stares at you, it means nothing.' I told her, 'Every single one of you needs to be treated at the hospital. Trachoma, parasites, smallpox, boils, and infections are festering in you.' They can't image a life without disease, but they avoid me because the dog has licked my ankle. The cavern . . . the cavern . . ."

I wrote, "Why do you bother with these people? Don't confront them. Let them be." I wrote, "It's me who will help you build your life; it's me who will bear you a healthy child." He answered: "In your opinion, you who live in the city and who will find someone else if I'm no longer around, in your opinion, why has that man buried his dagger in an animal's head, here, on the stone? There's an expression on the man's face that I don't understand. I can't stop looking at him. The expression has deepened as the stone has aged and peeled. His clenched teeth, the stone scar on his cheek . . ." I wrote, "For the love of whoever you care for, don't go to that cavern; you'll get sick." From his response, I knew he sneered when he read my letter . . . are you listening?

"Here, the weather is free from all seasons and here, all the dreams in the world settle like sediment. I close my eyes and I see them. Would you believe that a person's sense of smell can fantasize? It can, but just as we release our visual dreams by closing our eyes, we need to also free our fantasies of smell and sound. The dog and I sit facing the lines on the stone wall and then it starts to happen. The scent of a stream, the whiff of the honeybee's saliva, the smell of lean meat, the perfume of sweet blood in a vein, the smell of thunder, the aroma of an earthquake, the fragrance of a female . . ."

This must be his next letter, if I'm not mistaken—I didn't keep the envelopes. Starting with this one, even I had trouble reading his handwriting: "I told them, 'If you peek into my room again at night, in the middle of the night, I will go to the police and tell them all about the opium poppies you grow. Leave me alone.' They left me in peace for a while. But now they're picking on the dog. The animal is not that important to me. He's like all the other stray dogs that get hit by cars, their cadavers squashed by trucks. His left thigh has a sore and he constantly licks it, but that's not important. Maybe one of the dogs in the village bit him, but just because he bites off the scabs, it doesn't mean he's rabid. If he's not like other dogs, it doesn't mean he's rabid. Sabz-Ali confronted me: 'He is, he's rabid.' He said, 'Let's not tempt the devil; this year we've had no calamities.' The animal was sitting farther away, panting. Well, I feel hot and I pant, too, in this weather. Here, even stones pant; the air does, too. Rostam said, 'This dog is a stranger; he's not from Guraab or Gur-Gedaa. Our dogs are thin and agile. This one is like tame city dogs. There's no place for a strange dog in this village.' The day and the time had come; I didn't see that a few people had gathered around me; I only saw Rostam standing there, his neck stretched out. I wanted to tear out that protruding vein on his neck with my teeth, or with a fork. No matter how many times they kicked me in my side, I didn't let go of him. They were pulling my hair from behind and I was smashing Rostam's head against a rock and my hands were bloody and they separated us. I said, 'Leave the animal alone; I will kill him myself.' I even got the poison to smear on a goat's innards. The animal ate it. I threw it to him myself. He devoured the entire intestine and disappeared. It's now three days that I sit in the cavern alone. There's no more to say."

○○○○○

How does a man suddenly become like this? No, I never want to lay eyes on him again. He can go to wherever the hell he belongs to. But why did he waste three years of my life? I want to see him so that I can ask him just this. What a difference between the things he said at the beginning and the things he later wrote. What do I care if the dog didn't die from the poison, that he went back to him, still panting. He wrote: "The dog knows that I fed him poison, and he's come back to let me know this." This has to mean something. . . . What? Do you understand it? I don't know and I don't want to know what the animal in the stone carving—the one that resembles no other animal and yet bears a trait from all of them—actually is, or what it signifies. What does two thousand years ago or the return of the dog have to do with me? . . . The villagers saw the dog return. It managed to escape them and went to hide in the cavern. Maybe he hid the dog himself. I wouldn't put it past the person who wrote these letters. He wrote: "I will not let them be until I find out which one of us is genuine, which one of us is real. Hot bread and cheese, milking an animal, shimmering robes in a rhythmic dance, a gurgling spring, the music of a flute at dusk, they have all been shed from my fantasies like the filth on my body that peels off under my fingertips. Here, everything whirls around in a wind tunnel and turns into dust. The black shadows of the days, the darkness of the nights . . . They gnaw on dry bread; they steal if they can; like dogs, they hide their meager trifles from one another in a hundred little holes; they beat their wives at night and tell one another about it. . . .

"These same people raided my cavern, looking for the dog. I hadn't told them. I said I wouldn't tell. No one knew. I don't know how they found out. They dragged the poor animal outside with a rope. He didn't howl. He was docile. The rope squeezed his neck, but he did nothing. They pulled him up from the branch of a dead tree in the middle of the village. The children threw stones at him; they could have killed him then and there, but they wanted to torture me. They glared at me as they beat him with a stick and laughed when he thrashed about. . . . Now that I write, night has come and the dog is still hanging there. He's wheezing. I'm petrified of going out. He's probably calling me. He wants to stare at me with those sad eyes, like he always does. But I want to go to the image on the wall. I have discovered something. The animal is not attacking that man—the way he is standing on his hind legs, he doesn't look like an animal about to attack. He is the same height as the man and has rested his paws on the man's shoulders. Then why? . . . What do you think the shadow of a hanged dog looks like on a moonlit night? Try to see it in your sleep. Although I know you won't be able to hear the sounds."

I'm sure there was a lot of pain in his heart for him to take it out on me like this. It wasn't my fault if I couldn't understand what he was talking about and didn't know how to respond. And this is his last letter.

It wasn't written in sequence. There's no stamp on the envelope; it came with a package that had someone else's handwriting on it—a beginner's, a child's handwriting. Maybe the handwriting of someone he had taught to read and write. Perhaps he had spoken of me to this person, said things that made this person bring the package and leave it at our door one early morning. Early morning! That's how the letter begins.

"Early in the morning when I woke up, it was quiet everywhere. I had fallen asleep at midnight with the sound of the dog's rasps echoing in my ears. When I opened my eyes, I thought he must have choked to death by now. I looked out the window. The rope was still there, swaying in the wind, but there was no dog hanging from it. He had cut through the noose with his teeth. I laughed. I went over to the tree and laughed, and when Sabz-Ali came, I showed him the rope and laughed some more. One by one they came. They were terrified, and this made me laugh even harder. It seemed as though they were scared of me, too. Fearful of the rabid dog, they sent their wives and children home and, armed with shovels and clubs, they started searching high and low. . . . I'm going to look for the dog. . . ."

He wrote: "It's nighttime; no one dares leave his hut. On this hot and humid night, everyone has scurried into a hole. From afar the dog's wails circle Guraab, the wail of a wounded larynx that's still in the tight squeeze of a rope. My stomach is churning and I must sleep, but I'm not sleepy, and the minute I close my eyes, it's as if my nose and ears close up, too. And then they come—the smells, scenes, sounds, the sound of a dog's paws running over rocky ground, the pitch of a metal chisel carving stone, the roar of fire, the groan of a woman whose husband has bent her over like a dog, the hum of all the dreams in the world. I want to sleep, but my head won't let me. . . ."

There's more. Despite his dreadful state, he had written more: "I woke up with a start. It was him. I heard his paws on the window and the rasps of his constricted throat. I went to the window, but he was gone. I saw his shadow moving down the alleyway. This was the second night he had come to Guraab. Perhaps he was hungry. He stopped behind the door of a hut and rubbed his snout on it, as if he wanted to chew on the rotting wood. Somewhere a woman screamed. Everyone quickly put out their lanterns. Now they know that it's safer in the dark. There was the sound of a shout and then the dog's howl. In the morning, there were only a few drops of blood in front of the door of Farvardin's hut, nothing else. Farvardin says he aimed at the back of the dog's head with his gun, point-blank. But I'm sure he hasn't died. He will come again tonight. Even Farvardin stood in the middle of the road and yelled, 'If he comes back a thousand times, I will kill him a thousand times.' . . . Still, he will come. . . . Why won't he go away? What does he want to prove by staying in Guraab?" No, he seems to be writing much of this to himself or to others who will come after him, to others . . . not to me.

"It's finally over. Today was the second day after he lost his sixth life and escaped. I saw him when I left my room this morning. He was standing there under the same tree, panting and wagging his tail for me. Last night when he was howling under my window, I wished I had a gun so that I could kill him myself, so that we would all be rid of him. But someone in the alleyway shouted and again I heard a gunshot, and then there was silence, without a drop of blood on the ground. . . . What did the animal want from me, standing there as though nothing had happened. He was staring at me. I could see Sabz-Ali, armed with a shovel, tiptoeing toward him from behind. I saw him one step away from the dog, and he raised his shovel and the dog still stared at me. The shovel slid along his side and tore the skin off his back. He leaped toward me and ran into the alley. There, someone blocked his way and hit him with a club. He was foaming at the mouth. I'm sure. And he stopped wailing. Whichever direction he ran, someone appeared in front of him, and then he attacked. He wouldn't have attacked them if they had left him alone. The villagers poured out of their huts. Everyone was carrying something to beat the animal with. They pounded on his teeth. All that I have written are merely the howls that the dog never uttered, and now I'm at peace because I know I'm not real. They are the ones who exist; I only observe them, all of them. And the dog was evading their kicks and escaping to the hidden corners of the village. Froth, blood, and pandemonium. The dog's eyes were searching for me. There was a certain look in people's eyes as they screamed obscenities, chased him, and with all their might beat him with their shovels and clubs, and there was something about their frothing mouths, and just then, out of fear, I lost consciousness. The secret of the image in the cavern was being revealed to me and I could see that the bare teeth carved on the stone were a sign of these same teeth in foaming mouths and that the man was the ancient spirit of this rabid rage I saw before me. And I ran back toward the cavern, and amid the dust and screams and the howling of the wind, the dog, lame and butchered, was struggling to find an opening in the wall of flesh and blind blows. Just before reaching the hilltop, I fell, and there I turned around and looked back at Guraab.

"The helpless animal was lying on the ground; he had covered his eyes with his paws and the circle of flesh around him was getting tighter. Sabz-Ali approached him from the middle of the crowd and poured something on him. The animal didn't move. Perhaps they thought he was dead, and someone lit a match. Did that deafening howl not reach you? Perhaps you heard it somewhere among the folds and layers of the clamor in the city. If you were sitting in the garden at your house, which I once liked so much, and if the fountain in the shallow pool was on and the water bubbles were popping and the green leaves of the bitter orange tree were reflecting on the water, perhaps you heard the dog's cry as he went up in flames and leaped up and broke the circle of people and ran. Blind and engulfed in flames, he ran into a wall, he turned his head and reached for the flames around his middle and tried to bite at them, and leaving smoke and smell in his wake, he ran toward the wheat fields. I stumbled down the cavern stairs and lit a match. This was it; this was why it persistently dragged me to itself, captivated me. The magic of the carving is not in the image alone; it's also in its survival. And the man had plunged his dagger in the animal's head in such a way that it seems he had no other choice, and his face was turned toward me and he was looking at me and from between his clenched stone teeth he was growling something. His eyes, which were chipped at the corners and had taken on a beseeching look, said the same thing—'Strike.' And I picked up a stone and struck it against his teeth, just what he had been yearning for a thousand years. 'Shatter.' And I struck and struck again, stone against stone, and the stone cracked and crumbled and then there was darkness and the terrifying sound of water.

"When I left the cavern, the world was dark. Black smoke had enveloped Guraab and the plain. At the far end of the wheat fields, a few flames still rose amid the smoke. The people of Guraab, blackened, with singed hair and burned clothes, were on their knees here and there, staring at the black earth and sky. No one wept; no one moved. Rostam had piled up a small stack of wheat where he had first shown me his thirteen seeds. He had cut the stalks with his bare hands from in front of the fire. A woman held up her skirt filled with wheat . . . seeds for next year. No one saw me going toward my hut. . . . Now I feel weak. It is night and the smell of smoke bothers me. When I look out the window, out in the plain, ashes are still smoldering. It is good fertilizer for the soil, and I'm thinking how to seal this envelope, my mouth is so dry. . . ."

It must be morning. He hasn't written anything else. This is it, the end of his last letter. I don't know. No one has any news of him. Early one morning, someone left his few belongings behind our door. . . . I can't eat or sleep. Just a few nights ago, when everyone was asleep, I went and turned on a water faucet so that water slowly dripped from it, and then I lay down. The sound of the water grew louder and louder and little by little I thought I was hearing other sounds, too. . . . Sometimes I think, What if that dog dug its teeth into his flesh? Then I say, No, the dog wasn't rabid; an animal that docile wouldn't have turned wild for no reason. . . . But why didn't he understand that I was the one who was really there for him? After all that I've read to you, do you think I should wait for him? Do you think one day he will come, like he used to, or no . . . has he gone for good?

Seasons of Purgatory

JUST LIKE THAT, HE STAYED AND STAYED and days and nights in succession passed. His clothes decayed, the trichina grew gaunt on his flesh, the sun sapped his fat, and the earth around him turned slimy and black. One day, we noticed that his lips had decomposed—it was the worms' doing—his long teeth were exposed; he looked like he was laughing. Late one night, an animal ripped off his arm and took it away, but he didn't fall. Leaning against a rock, just like that, he stayed and stayed. . . . The old hands left, the enlisted arrived, and the wind took away his putrid stench and the hair on his skull and brought autumn clouds. Rainwater gathered in mortar craters, and the skeleton, still there, with his eye sockets stared at the earth. . . . Snow fell and covered him. We thought that was the end, but the sun grew warm again and melted the snow. Grass sprouted from the earth, chamomile, wild poppy, and all kinds of spring flowers. . . .

Weeds had crept up in between his ribs by the time we told and retold all of this to our new commanding officer; some of us may not have been able to tell it all from beginning to end. Some of us are illiterate, many have only a third- or fourth-grade education, a few have high school degrees; some weren't even around to see that day of reckoning. And so, if we all tell the story, if we tell it together, it's as though we have told it all, and the newly arrived lieutenant would stare at our lips and light one cigarette after another. He would say, "I don't understand . . . I don't understand what it all means, but why for so long?" And we would say, "Sir, once we tell the story, you will understand. To us, he's not just a dried-up skeleton." And the lieutenant would constantly come up with excuses to go and look at the valley floor. He would ask, "Didn't you say that when it's a full moon, his skull shines? Then why don't I see it? . . . Didn't you say that every so often his head is turned to a different side? Then why is it that ever since I arrived, his face has been turned toward his ripped-out arm?" We'd say, "Be patient, Lieutenant, it hasn't even been a week since you arrived. Didn't Captain Meena tell you that your eyes have to get used to this place for you to see what others don't?" But the lieutenant would look at us as though we were different from other soldiers.

Captain Meena was a good commanding officer. He knew how to fight. He'd been at the front for five years; he didn't count the days until he could go on leave. A few months after Nasser's corpse came to stay, he stopped going on leave altogether. Every twenty or thirty days, he'd go to town for a bath and return at night. On the night he left, he had told the lieutenant replacing him, "I didn't put in a transfer request. It was better for me here; I could understand what I turned into. . . . Why did they transfer me to the rear?" . . . One night when the truck brought our rations, we saw the lieutenant climb out of it. Tall and lanky . . . For no good reason, he flashed a smile at everyone he passed. Here, it's unbecoming to laugh. His clothes were pressed and his face hadn't seen the sun. We pretty much ignored him. We figured he was just another visiting officer from headquarters. But then we saw Captain Meena briefing him. He showed him the rocky hill across the valley and all the positions where the enemy had set up observation posts. He familiarized him with the infiltration points of our camp and the locations where we didn't have clear fields of fire. Then the lieutenant's eyes were glued to the valley floor. It was as if he were staring into the pits of hell. Captain Meena laughed and said, "Oh . . . He's here, too. He's been with us for a while. . . . His name is Nasser. . . ." And again he laughed.

Captain Meena's voice had been hoarse ever since the previous winter. His laugh sounded like the cough of an old man who had smoked Oshnou cigarettes all his life. If a stranger heard it, it would raise the hair on the back of his neck. The sergeant major had told us that the minute the captain fell asleep, something blocked his throat. His breathing was like that of people with diphtheria and he barked out orders in his sleep. "Open fire. . . . Don't let them off. . . . Move it. . . ." And so he would sleep all day, and at night he would wander around the observation post trenches. The duty officer had heard him tell the lieutenant not to let the soldiers come out during the day. "The sixty-millimeter mortars come as quietly as the Angel of Death. . . . Other than the watch guards and the duty officer, make everyone sleep during the day and stay up at night. Although, as long as Nasser is down there, I doubt the Iraqis will have the guts to move in on us." We told the lieutenant, "Don't look at Captain Meena's bent back and worn-out body. You should have seen him on that day of combat, you should have seen him." And we said, "That day at the crack of dawn, the captain had just gone to sleep when we heard a couple of rounds from a Kalashnikov being fired on the rocky hill. One of our patrol guards randomly emptied a few rounds while the duty officer ran over to Captain Meena's dugout. Even those of us who were sleeping heard the captain holler, 'Every man to front-line trenches.'

"Near dawn, between sleep and wakefulness, Kalashnikov shots in the mountain sound like toy guns popping. You can't believe those silly bang bangs have just then ripped through flesh and shattered bone. Then, it was still dark in the valley—the night takes long leaving it—but you could see a white handkerchief waving down there. The watch guard pointed it out to Captain Meena with the barrel of his rifle. Just then, someone shouted, 'Captain! . . . Captain! . . .' The captain shouted back, 'I see them, too.' Three or four shadows were climbing over the rocky hill and moving down toward the darkness of the valley. From inside the observation post, the captain ordered, 'Open fire,' and he leaped out. Before the guns went off, we heard that wounded howl from the valley floor. It was louder than any gun.

"Then you heard nothing. All those rifles being fired, the heavy machine guns, mortars exploding . . . and the sound of these, too, you couldn't hear, because your ears were full and it seemed like there was only Captain Meena in your head, yelling, 'Fire at the rocky hill. . . . Look. . . . Fire . . . fire wherever you see muzzle flashes. . . .' And all across the dusty haze of the rocky hill we saw muzzle flashes from rifles and heavy machine guns. . . . We didn't understand how their bullets passed over our trenches and our heads, and we felt our own rifles recoil. . . . One touch to the trigger and seven or eight bullets flew out, and from the other side, too, seven or eight came your way, and you thought, Now, right now, the force of a bullet will throw me back . . . but it will take a while. Most times it took a while, and suddenly the mortar shells came. . . ."

The lieutenant, who had never seen combat, would listen carefully. We thought, He probably wants to know what combat is like and what he has to do, and we thought, Let's tell him so that he knows, so that next time, when the time comes, and it will, he will at least not flip out. We told him, "The first incoming mortars usually fall short or pass far overhead, and two mortars landed together right in the middle of the camp. Captain Meena was yelling, 'Ammo . . . ammo . . .' Under mortar fire, it takes a lot of guts to carry ammunition to the trenches. . . . Kaagoli, bless his memory . . . he never refused. He was from the north. His name made everyone laugh. He was a duty officer. He would hear Captain Meena's order and he'd run off to obey it, whether it was his duty or not. That's why he was the captain's favorite. He would carry the ammo boxes on his back from trench to trench . . . and we recklessly emptied the clips and belts, and the buzzing bees were above our heads, one hundred bees . . . two hundred bees . . . there was no end to it. We seemed to have forgotten that it was all because of that damned Nasser, trapped at the bottom of the valley, waving his white handkerchief and screaming . . . from fear, from pain . . . from . . . from who knows what. . . . We weren't the ones stuck down there with all hell breaking loose around us. We and the Iraqis had trenches and shelters, we weren't alone, but poor Nasser . . . The Iraqis would lower their barrels and shower the rock he was taking cover behind with bullets. . . .

"'Radio Ops . . . Radio Ops . . . encode headquarters . . . encode ammunitions . . .' The field radio operator would stick a finger in one ear and yell, 'This is Simorgh . . . this is Simorgh . . .'

"'Radio Ops, encode ambulance . . .'

"'Alborz . . . come in, Alborz . . . this is Simorgh . . .'

"Kaagoli told the captain we'd had a few wounded. They had pulled three of our guys out from under the rubble of a trench, covered in blood and dirt. Next to the trench there was now a small crater; the earth was smoldering in its belly. The captain had barely made it over there when he threw himself on top of the wounded. Those who were there heard the howl of the shrapnel. It was a close one. The guys' faces were black with soot. And then one of the wounded under the captain's body started to convulse and his blood was pouring down the captain's collar. . . . We dragged the wounded over to the field medics' trench and went back to the hilltop. The sun had come up, but smoke and dust had swallowed up the earth and the sky and we couldn't see what the man with the handkerchief was doing. A soldier yelled, 'I can't see. . . . I can't see.' And suddenly there was quiet everywhere. The guns were all silent. Someone said, 'I got two of them.' Someone else said, 'I sent one of their observation posts flying with an RPG.' And then, we didn't know from where, a single shot was fired, and it all started again. . . .

"Kaagoli told us that the captain kept trying to see Nasser through his binoculars, but he couldn't. In all that smoke and dust, he couldn't distinguish him from rocks and dirt . . . and Kaagoli was the first one to see that the observation watch guard had dropped to the ground and was clinging onto the captain's leg, screaming, 'Captain . . . Captain . . .' Captain Meena hadn't noticed and was telling the gunner where to fire. When he looked down and saw, he clutched the watch guard's chest. By the time the medics came, blood was gushing out from between the captain's fingers. The captain pried the watch guard's hand from around his wrist so that they could take him away. As they carried him off, the watch guard kept calling 'Captain Meena,' as if the captain's name would heal his wound. . . .

"That's what the captain was to the guys. Like a rock you could take shelter behind. Even if ten of us were shot dead, he wouldn't lose his cool. Later, he changed. He became more and more of a loner and we saw less and less of him, and if we did, it was in the middle of the night, when he would quietly walk past the watch-guard trenches, like a hunchbacked shadow, and he would tap his bayonet against the rocks and the sandbags ... *thump* ... *thump* ... *thump* ... and he would fade into the dark. Week after week, we saw him become more haggard, just as on the valley floor Nasser's flesh was becoming more sallow. We watched him when we were on guard duty.

"Two hours of guard duty during the day, three hours at night, with nothing to do but watch and think; and we kept thinking, and when a friend would ask, 'What are you thinking about?' we wouldn't say; though if we asked him, he wouldn't breathe a word, either. And at night, in the middle of the night, one of us would jolt awake, drenched in sweat, and he would listen to see whether he'd heard that scream in his sleep or whether someone in the valley was calling for help. We all knew what sort of a dream he'd had—the sort that Captain Meena would have just before dawn and he would shout, 'Red alert,' and he would drag us out to the front-line trenches with weapons armed, fingers on the trigger, and eyes glued to the rocky hill, which in the white of dawn seemed dark and loomed like a bloated, dead monster. And we would stand ready in the trenches without seeing any movement other than that of the sun spreading across the valley, and Nasser's corpse, which emerged from the dark just as it had been. ..."

By the time we got to this point, the lieutenant would be furious. He would shove his cigarette butt into a hole in our trench and growl, "I don't get it. . . . Why . . . what happened to you and Captain Meena? . . . The way you all behave . . . the things you say makes one think . . . it's as if Nasser is present on every inch of this hill. . . . It's as if you . . ." The guys would laugh at him and then suddenly grow silent, meaning, You're new and you still haven't had a piece of molten shrapnel fly past the base of your head. You haven't shot even one Iraqi. What do you really understand? . . . And the lieutenant would clumsily crawl out on all fours, in a way that either his torso or his head would get stuck in the entranceway. He was just not army material. At night in the trenches, the guys would gather around and say, "With this kind of a commander, let's pray to God that we don't come under attack. Otherwise, not one of us will walk out of here alive."

The lieutenant always talked to the sergeant major about the gillyflowers in his garden at home and wrote letters at night . . . who knows to whom, to his wife, to someone else . . . whoever she was. Close to going on leave, he would pine for her and, like a miserable orphan, he would huddle in a corner and count the hours. Captain Meena wasn't like that. Although, after Nasser came, he did become bad-tempered; the minute someone misbehaved, the captain would give him disciplinary guard duty or extend his term of service. But his presence alone was everything to us. It was as if all there was in this world was this hill and him. This past year, he went to his town only once, and when he came back, the sergeant major told Kaagoli that the captain and his wife had split up. . . . It's true that there's a lot we don't understand, but we know we should never ask, we should never ask a man who has been at the front for five years why his wife has left him . . . and he never asked us why we were eating less, why we didn't joke around like we used to, why we weren't eager to go on leave. . . .

Sometimes the veteran soldiers made fun of the lieutenant. That first night when he arrived, the lieutenant was standing next to the observation post, staring at the valley floor. One of the soldiers quietly crept up to him and suddenly burst into laughter. Startled, the lieutenant leaped up and yelled, "Why are you laughing like this?" He shouted, "Why do you all laugh like Captain Meena?" The soldier said, "Sir, I just wanted to tell you that if you stare down there at night, the stones and rocks will all start to look like bones." . . . And again the lieutenant would come over and ask, "So what happened next?" He sounded like a soldier who had fought to the last ounce of his energy and had given up; and we would say over and over again that in the middle of combat you don't feel time pass.

"At some point, we looked up and realized that it was almost noon and it was quiet everywhere. The smoke and dust had settled, the wind had carried away the sweet smell of gunpowder and mortar primers, and then we saw the valley floor. Behind the rock, hunched over, the Iraqi soldier had taken cover, facing us. . . . We thought he was probably dead because he wasn't moving; he was still holding his white handkerchief. From the top of the rocky hill, they fired a single shot at him. It hit the rock and ricocheted. They wouldn't leave him alone. Captain Meena handed the binoculars to Kaagoli and said, 'See if the guy is moving or not.' He patted Kaagoli on the back and went over to the field medics' trench to reassure the wounded. . . . We managed to carry the wounded through the ravine behind us and to the ambulances that were waiting two kilometers away. We distributed bread and dates to all the trenches, drank some water—thirst is worse than injury—loaded the clips, and were leaning against the sandbags when the wailing started. The sky was gloomy and bleak, the sun was hot and hazy, and the Iraqi soldier hadn't died.

"He was howling and waving his handkerchief at us. The handkerchief was no longer white; it was red, blotchy. Captain Meena said, 'Night . . . if he makes it until nighttime, they'll come and put him out of his misery.' But at noon prayers, the wounded man's cries tore into our faith. The cry for 'Water . . . water . . .' traveled to the trench where we were resting. Some of us covered our ears, some of us started to talk loudly, but we could still hear him. Kaagoli said that during lunch, the minute the captain came to take a bite, his eyes caught sight of his nails. They were black underneath—not black, red black. The watch guard's blood had dried under the captain's nails. He threw down his food and climbed out of the trench. His shout echoed everywhere, 'Water only for drinking . . . conserve.'

"The boxes of ammo were scattered all over the place, the ground around the heavy machine guns was littered with empty shells, and the soldiers' eyes looked like they'd been sprayed with blood. Captain Meena used to say, 'Now you've become combat soldiers; whoever makes it out of this battlefield can be called a man.' And we just watched Nasser. We couldn't throw anything to him, and he couldn't move from behind the rock. They'd shoot him if he moved. He had no way forward and no way back, and there was fighting on both sides. Then the sergeant major lost it; he aimed his rifle at Nasser and said, 'Listen to how the miserable bastard howls. . . . Captain, shall I put him out of his misery?' And the Arab was constantly screaming. We couldn't understand his language, but we could tell he was begging. Maybe he wanted us to take him out—his arm was always stretched out toward us. We thought, When someone is thrashing about in agony all day in front of us, we have to do something, and we didn't know what to do. Wounds make you thirsty, fear makes you thirsty, just sitting and thinking makes you thirsty. Up in the sky, a bird had spread its wings and was circling above the wounded man, and the wounded man was clawing at the earth. One of the soldiers heard Captain Meena tell the sergeant major, 'He's ruining the guys' morale.' And the sergeant major said, 'So far, we've sustained four wounded for this blasted Arab. . . .

Shall I take him out?' And we heard him yell from the fire step of the trench, 'Shut up, bastard! . . .' Captain Meena took the sergeant major's rifle and unloaded it.

"The sandbags had gotten hot and a scorching wind gusted through the observation loopholes and into our eyes. We wanted to see the wounded man's face. He was the first Iraqi we had seen this close. We always saw them as shadows along the ridge and they vanished into the mountain as soon as we fired mortar shells. But we couldn't see his face. He was writhing and thrashing about in a bad way. From inside the trench, Captain Meena called out to him, 'Snake your way up . . . snake your way . . .' We yelled, 'Climb up . . . come on up, you coward.' The captain shouted, 'Hey . . . do you understand our language?' And he said something in Arabic. The wind carried fragments of his words, and it seemed as though our voices didn't travel beyond the trench. Again we yelled, 'What's your name . . . hey . . . your name?' And just then we thought, What in the world does this mean? He was answering. It sounded like he was saying, 'Nasser . . .' We all yelled together, 'Climb up! . . . Nasser, climb up!' Nasser stretched one leg out, and instantly a sniper's bullet plunged into the dirt right next to it. They were lying in ambush for him at every turn. We figured he was about to die. The bird had moved down closer. Just then, a timed mortar exploded above the valley. Its shrapnel flew against the rocks around us. They wanted to kill him no matter what. Another mortar exploded in the air. The bird flew away and two stacks of black smoke swelled in the sky. From one of the trenches someone threw a plastic water cask down toward the valley floor. It landed a hundred meters away from the wounded man and rolled down. The Iraqi's howls stopped. It was just then that the captain managed to see the man's face through his binoculars. Later he told us, he told us that the man was staring at the cask. He was thin and olive-skinned, like all Arabs. He had a mustache and his bald spot shined under the sun. Then a few bursts of machine-gun fire came from the rocky hill and the cask burst. The captain came out and yelled, 'Who threw the cask?' Kaagoli said, 'Me.' The captain yelled, 'One extra week of service. . . . Don't you know that you shouldn't give water to a wounded man?' Kaagoli said, 'What difference does it make, Captain? What difference does it make?'"

The lieutenant, too, would ask, "What difference could it have made for the poor man?" And we'd say we didn't know. Then he would suddenly ask, "Did you guys start playing this game after Nasser came?" We'd say, "Yes," and we'd think, Lieutenant, you don't understand. You haven't had Nasser in front of you for an entire year. How would you know what our pastime means. And it isn't even a game. It's a test. We pull the safety pin out of a hand grenade and, holding down the safety lever, we clutch the grenade in our fist to see who can hold it longer. Two hours . . . three hours . . . if your hand weakens even a tiny bit, the fuse could activate; most times you won't even hear it, but three seconds later . . . *boom!* . . . in your hand . . .

Anyone who is weak, his hand will start to shake after a while, but if he lasts, after he puts the safety pin back in and unclenches his fist, he'll be a different man. . . . The lieutenant struggled for two weeks to get us to quit this habit, but he was no match for us. How long could he go on with his surprise visits to our trenches in the middle of the night? Even if he inspected all the trenches, he wouldn't have the guts to check all the twists and turns in the hill . . . so he finally gave up.

At the time, we couldn't understand why he insisted that we keep telling him the story. We thought perhaps he wanted us to remember things that we had not yet told him. But we could tell he was staring into our eyes, hoping to read our minds. By then, his own eyes had sunken in his face, he didn't shave regularly anymore, he'd grown skinnier, and he had stopped writing letters. And we'd say, "Lieutenant, you should have seen Kaagoli. He was fair, well built, and his smile never left his lips. . . . A few times he flexed his arm and threw bandages down to the wounded guy. But they didn't reach him, and the man's screams changed—they sounded like the squeals of a mouse when you put your foot on his bloated belly and push down until it bursts. Then Kaagoli told Captain Meena, 'Captain, let's do something, let's do something to stop him from getting this way.' The captain said, 'What would you suggest I do? . . . It can't be done. . . . He's no longer an enemy. He stopped being our enemy when he set out and walked toward us. . . .' Then he turned to the soldiers watching him. 'This is it. . . . Stuff something in your ears. This is what war is. . . .' He yelled at Kaagoli, 'What is it you want me to do? . . . Don't give me that sourpuss look.' And he went to his dugout, alone. . . .

"As long as the sun was up, the watch guards kept an eye on Nasser with their binoculars and told us about him. He reached over, pulled out a dried-up bush, and chewed on its root. Then he tore his shirt and bandaged his wound. A few times, it looked like he was steeling himself to get up, but he fell. They shot at him. He crouched down behind the rock, and by dusk his cries were weaker, and when it got darker, there was no sound at all. The rations truck arrived with its lights turned off. It had brought ammunition and letters. No one felt like opening the letters. We wanted the moon to come out. A full moon. Maybe it would make it eas- ier to pass the night, and the wounded guy in the valley could gaze at it until all his blood finally drained. But the night was dark and Nasser started to scream again. It sounded like he wasn't begging anymore. He was cursing. . . . The sergeant major paced up and down and said, 'That damn Arab has seven lives.'"

Amazed, the lieutenant would ask, "Are you sure he hadn't died yet?" And we'd say, "Yes, we're sure. A sound like the sound of a jackal echoed in the valley. Some of the soldiers say he sometimes called out a woman's name. Maybe he was calling his mother." Then a few of us would take the lieutenant over to the obser- vation post to show him. "Look here, Lieutenant, when you arrived three months ago, weren't his eye sock- ets turned toward his armless shoulder? Now he has turned; he's looking at his ribs." He would say, "Maybe the wind turned his head." And we'd say, "No . . . we've kept an eye on him for a year now. We've seen what has gradually happened to him. The animals chewed his clothes so that they could get to his flesh. . . . His nose fell . . . see! His boots are still intact and you can see his shiny dog tags on his ribs. . . . You've probably seen the late-afternoon winds. When the wind starts, there are whirlwinds down there in the valley; all the whirlwinds come up from between his ribs. . . . It's nonsense what they say about men missing a left rib."

And the lieutenant, looking like he was about to vomit, would climb out of the observation post. But at night he'd come back, like the walking dead, and he would ask, "This Captain Meena . . . didn't you say he really looked out for his soldiers? Then how could he have let you make a move toward Nasser that night?" We would say, "Perhaps he just blurted it out. . . . When he said, 'Now it's dark enough for the Iraqis to go down to Nasser,' we asked him what they would do to him. The captain said they would treat his wounds, interrogate him, and then execute him. . . . Kaagoli said, 'I'll go get him.' And the captain blurted out, 'If you find two other volunteers, I won't object.' Maybe he thought we were tired and no one would volunteer. But fifteen minutes later, three guys, all geared up, were standing at his dugout. The captain only said, 'Be careful when you get close. He may shoot at you,' and he radioed headquarters.

"Kaagoli and the other two started moving down.

For a while we could hear the sound of stones skipping out from under their feet, and then we only heard the groans of the wounded guy. We were thinking that when they brought Nasser up, we'd straight away ask him how many troops were positioned behind the rocky hill and where their fucking mortars were. . . . And then we suddenly realized the Iraqi was quiet. We figured they had reached him. Then we saw the flame. It looked like someone had lit a match down there, and noise exploded in the valley. The muzzle flashes increased. We thought, Damn, they've engaged the Iraqi patrols. Panicked, Captain Meena yelled, 'Don't shoot at the valley floor. . . . Hit the slope of the hill.' From inside the canal on top of the hill, the Iraqis started shooting, too, and again the buzz of the bees was all around us. Tracer bullets, bright red, slashed through the sky. We were yelling, 'Guys, climb up . . . climb up!' We had no idea that we were showering the Iraqis' draw-back line with bullets and they were doing the same to the return route of our patrols. . . . It seemed as if whoever went down there would have no way out and would stay there forever. Captain Meena had run over to the fifty-millimeter. His entire bulk shook from the recoils of the heavy machine gun. He was swinging the barrel left and right and swearing. Bent shadows were running all around us, sparks flew as the bullets hit the rocks. Men were shouting and rifles and machine guns with scorching barrels that wouldn't melt were relentlessly firing.

"A tracer bullet detonated in the air. Like a torch with no hand holding it, it slowly came down and the wind carried it toward the valley. Its glow cast trembling shadows along the sides of the valley. We figured if they'd shot a tracer, then the Iraqi patrols must have retreated. They wanted to see our patrols. We aimed at the tracer to shoot it down. The smell of gunpowder burned our lungs and the dust particles from the bullets got into our eyes. Captain Meena kept shouting, 'Move back, Kaagoli . . . climb up. . . .' Then right next to the fifty-millimeter there was a groan, and someone crawled up and collapsed on the ground. The captain knelt down and asked, 'Who is it?' They told him it was Kaagoli. The captain ran his hand over Kaagoli's head and chest—even in the dark you can feel the wetness and warmth of blood. The captain raised his hand up to his eyes. Kaagoli rolled over. The bullet had exited from his side. The captain pressed his fist on Kaagoli's wound, looked up at the torch falling from the sky, and roared."

We told the lieutenant, "That was it, just that. We evacuated Kaagoli to the rear and we have no more news of him." We said, "That night until dawn, there was thirst on our lips and sleep that burned in our eyes; and in the morning, it was morning and the Iraqi defector, peaceful, with his legs and arms spread wide open, was leaning against the rock with his head slumped down on his chest; and at noon, it was noon and a vulture was sitting on Nasser's stomach, plucking out his eyes; and at night, it was again night and the squeal of the mice rose from the valley. And this is how it was for many days and nights, for many dawns and dusks." And we said, "In spite of everything, we're used to him; he's one of us. We fought for him an entire day and night; we sustained casualties. And he, too, struggled for an entire day and night to reach us. So now, what difference does it make where he is, on the valley floor or in a grave? What's important is that he is. We carry with us the image of what he lived through that day. The same way that Captain Meena couldn't forget and at night would wander around this hill and his shadow would fall across the valley floor. We still hear the clanking of his bayonet against the rocks and sandbags."

And this was the last time we told the story to the lieutenant. With his face gaunt and his eyes bloodshot and sleepless, he sat staring at the flame of the oil lamp, waiting, waiting as though there was more to say. And then he went to his dugout and we didn't see him for two whole days. . . . The morning of the third day, he suddenly called a stand-to alert. He yelled, "To front-line trenches, move it!" We wondered what was going on; perhaps we were under attack. We quickly loaded our rifles, but there was no movement on the rocky hill. Then we saw the lieutenant stagger over and kneel down next to the observation post. He was holding an RPG. He lifted it up to his shoulder and released the safety catch. That first-day smile was back on his lips. He patiently aimed and fired. The sound of the explosion echoed in the mountain, dust and smoke rose from the valley floor, and there was no sign left of Nasser and his rock. The lieutenant straightened his back and said out loud, "May God rest his soul."

If She Has No Coffin

THE MORNING SUN PEEKING OVER THE WALL had bright-
ened half of the sour orange tree in the garden
patch. Among its leaves, Dorna again saw the fruits left
over from last year. "Just like shiny jewels," she said.
And Sara, who, according to what Father had said that
morning, was dead, did not as usual say, "No . . . like
fire . . ." There was a large crisscross across the small
garden and the wall behind it. A long time ago, Sara
had tried to scratch the tape off the window with her
fingernails, but it had not come off.

Father walked in and said, "My girl, I have to take
Sara away now."

Dorna cried. She wanted to go with him, just like
the day Father had said Sara was sick and she had gone
with them as far as the door to the doctor's office.

"Don't do this," Mother said. "Do you realize what
you're doing? Don't do it."

"It's something I started. . . . I have to finish it. . . .
It's better this way. . . . My girl, you stay home."

Dorna screamed, "It was you and Mom who wanted
her to die. You two. Mom didn't take care of her at all.
So now, I'm going with you!"

"Where to?" Father said. "Do you know where I'm
going? Look, I'll take Sara away and I'll be right back.

I'll take her somewhere . . . I don't know, I'll ask around and take her somewhere that's right for her."

Mother sat down on a chair and said, "What are you doing! . . . At least not like this."

"I'm going, too! No matter what, I'm going with you."

"Where to?" Father shouted. "To the cemetery? You want to go to the cemetery?"

Dorna ran to the door. . . . Father finally gave in.

"I won't say anything anymore," Mother moaned. "I'm done."

Dorna put on her street clothes and walked out with Father.

"Is the cemetery far?" she asked.

"It's very far," he said. "But now that you want to come with me, we'll walk all the way there."

Father rubbed his hands together hard. Then he wrung them as though there were soap on his fingers and he wanted to spread it all over. Dorna's eyes were still wet when they reached the main street. Father stopped and stared ahead.

"Why did Sara die?" Dorna asked.

"How many times are you going to ask me this? She didn't listen. She was stubborn. It was cold and she went out to the yard without her coat; she got sick. . . . This is what happens to children who don't listen to what grown-ups tell them."

"Then, me, too?"

The city was again being bombed. The street was

empty. Most of the shops were closed and only now and then a car sped by.

Father said, "I'm telling you now, you are not allowed to go inside the cemetery. Do you understand? You are not allowed. When we get there, don't start crying and screaming that you want to go inside."

"Later, after you bury her, can we put flowers on her grave like we do for Grandmother?"

Father took her hand and they crossed the street. Most of the buildings had the same crisscrossed tape on their windows, but in different colors.

Dorna asked, "So why didn't I die when I had a cold?"

It seemed Father didn't hear her. He kept looking left and right, and then he looked up at the sky. Dorna asked again. Father didn't answer. Dorna asked again. And Father said, "Sara was very sick. Last week the doctor said she was terribly ill. But it's all right. You shouldn't be sad. She's gone to heaven. She's happy. . . . She's playing with the angels."

"Are there schools in heaven?"

"No."

"So Sara's happy. Really happy! Right? She didn't like doing homework, either, just like me."

She wanted to say, "I wish I would die, too." But she knew Father would shout, "What is it that you don't have in your life? Haven't your mother and I sacrificed enough so that you would have everything?" And he would yell even louder, "Sara, you ungrateful, unkind girl, you do nothing but torment us. Stop teaching these things to Dorna." And the door would slam shut and she would hear Mother say, "Stop going on and on about Sara this and Sara that; it'll make things worse. Can't you understand . . . she has started to actually talk to Sara." And Father would say, "She's comparing. . . . She's starting to understand the difference between good and bad."

And Dorna wondered what Sara would do just then, if she were alive. She would probably leap into the street and run against traffic, screaming, "Honk 'til you drop dead!" Or perhaps she would go on the grass divider and not listen to Father, not even when the knees of her cherry red pants turned green. She would not listen to Father at all, and she would force him to buy things for her. Even if Father said he had no money, she would still force him to buy whatever she suddenly craved. She would tell him he was a bad Father because he had no money, and she would cry, she would cry as much as she wanted, and she would cry in front of strangers, and she wouldn't care that it was wrong for a big girl to cry like that in front of people. And then she would say, "I wish all the people on the street would die, all the muggers, so that we can go out, all the shopkeepers, so that we can take whatever we want, all the airplanes, all the school principals . . . and I wish only that old man would stay alive."

"Maybe Sara isn't dead."

Father growled between his teeth, "She's dead."

"If she's not dead and you bury her, it'll hurt her. She'll be cold when it snows in the winter. And it'll be your fault . . . and Mother's. She never gave her any lunch."

Father stopped, lit a cigarette, and nervously flung the matchstick behind him. The blare of the red-alert siren rose in the distance. A car pulled over alongside the street gutter. The driver got out and huddled down next to the car. Father yanked Dorna by the arm and started to run. He stopped . . . looked around. He dragged her across the street and they ran up the stairs in front of a tall building. Behind the closed doors, they could hear someone running. Father pounded on the door. They heard footsteps descending the stairs. No one opened the door. Father held Dorna in his arms and crouched over her. If Sara were there, she would have escaped his arms and run into the street to see where the bombs were falling, and Father would have shaken his arms in the air and shouted at the people, "Damn you! A bombed house is nothing to watch; a corpse is nothing to gawk at!"

Dorna said, "Dad, let's go back home."

"It'll be over soon," Father whispered. "Don't be afraid. . . . It's nothing. It'll stop."

Through the crook of Father's elbow, Dorna could see a white cloud gently floating in the air. The sky was blue. Like the blue of the sea in paintings, and the cloud was so bright that it hurt her eyes. Father's smell bothered her. He smelled like that every time he got angry with Sara and yelled at her. The day Sara plucked all the violets in the garden patch and Father saw their petals on the floor, in the middle of the room, Dorna had quickly said, "Sara did it." When Father grabbed Sara by the arm and took her to the garden and spanked her right there, the smell was worse than ever. It was like the smell of dirty socks. The white-alert siren went off. Dorna knew the bombs had the habit of falling more at night. Father took her hand and they set off.

"You always scolded her," Dorna said. "Let's buy a few candies and leave them next to her."

"The dead . . ."

And he didn't finish his sentence. The war anthem was being broadcast from a loudspeaker. When they reached it, there was a lot of commotion on the street, and after they were some distance away, again the street was quiet and empty. Dorna looked up at the cloud. If only it would come down and make everything white, so white that it would hurt their eyes and Father would close his eyes, and she and Sara could run away. She was sorry she had gotten scared the night Sara wanted to run away. What had Sara done that day? She couldn't remember. Perhaps she had peed in the garden patch while standing up, as she often did. All Dorna could remember was that Sara was locked up in her room again. . . . The neighborhood's old hunchback was walking toward them. Now and then he stopped, held up his cane like a rifle, and pretended to shoot at the people and the cars. Father let go of Dorna and again wrung his hands, as if he were holding them under a faucet and rinsing off soapsuds. Then he looked at her and smiled, and Dorna smiled back and grabbed the hem of his long jacket.

Father said, "For Sara . . . Are you listening to me, my

girl? I want to tell you a secret. A big secret, just between you and me . . . Perhaps for Sara . . . How should I put it? . . . You can't tell anyone our secret. This is a secret between three people, because . . . Well, now that Sara is gone, it's a secret between two people. Yes, between you and me. Perhaps Sara is gone because she wanted to go, because it was better for her. And she didn't listen to you and me because she didn't love us. . . . Don't you think it's better for her this way? It's what she wanted. This world wasn't good for her. Where she is now? . . . Well, let's just say, it's better for her. . . . Don't you think so?"

"No."

Father took Dorna's hand. His palm was sweaty. The scent of sour orange blossoms had filled the air.

"It was better for her. She wanted it this way. Now it's just your mother and me and our one and only daughter, who is a very good girl. Daddy adores her because she is a very, very good girl."

"There are no kids at all on the street," Dorna said.

Father was still talking. His voice was gentle and kind. Dorna had not listened to most of what he had said.

"Now you have to accept the fact that Sara isn't here anymore. . . ."

Dorna thought, If all the children are dead, like Sara, they are probably having a lot of fun together in heaven. She snatched at the air and clenched her fist to hold on to the scent of sour orange blossoms.

Father asked, "Would you like to go out for a walk tonight?"

Whenever they went out, Sara would stop and stare at people, in the park, on the sidewalk. Father would pull her by the hand. Sara always wanted to stop and watch when men got into a fight. They probably got into fights everywhere. But Father would drag her away. Sara didn't like it when as soon as they saw people standing on line somewhere, they had to go and stand there, too, and use their coupon to get cooking oil. Father would grab her hand and hold her there, and Sara would scream, "We don't want this oil! It's pissy oil." And at night, from behind the window, Mother would watch her tear at the soil in the garden patch and grab fistfuls of dry, curled-up sour orange leaves and throw them up in the air. . . . But Mother was against Sara's being there; from the very start, she didn't want her to exist. The night's garden was blue when Father said, "I know my girl knows what's right. And I know who tricks her, tricks her into not doing as she's told." Dorna had asked, "If you think you know, then tell me who it is." And Father had replied, "Sara . . . a mean and naughty Sara, who sits with you and whispers things in your ear." Mother had screamed from outside, "Don't say these things!" And then their fights had become more regular. More regular than when Dorna's brother, who was in Mother's stomach, didn't come out, and Auntie said, "The child was miscarried from the shock of these bombs." And in the kitchen, Mother would say, "Don't do this. My child will only get worse." And out in the yard, shadows would rise from the ground and Father would say, "You don't understand anything. If you did, you would have raised her so that she wouldn't break the window at school. You can't even make her wash her hands and face." And Mother would scream and call Father stupid and crazy, and Father would come outside and say, "Bad Sara can go do whatever the heck she wants, but my Dorna will sit down and do her homework, and tomorrow she will grab the top grade from these mean, stingy lessons that want my girl to be lazy and not do well." And Dorna, scared by his voice that didn't sound as it usually did, would sit at her desk to write her homework, and she would see Sara drawing pictures on the wall with all the colors of her pencils, and in between the colors she would write: *airplane* . . . write: *death to* . . . write: *3+1=S*. And she would see Sara biting the blond doll's hand, and she would hear Father calling out, "Are you writing, Dorna?" And she would reply, "Yes." And Sara would stare out the window at the garden's night. "Write, Dorna!" And Sara would pass through the glass, and out in the yard; she would gather all the shadows, pile them up in the middle of the garden patch, and kick them. The shadows of all the mean people who lied and pretended to be Father's friends. And Father would walk in, and because Sara had not written anything, he would grab her notebook and throw it out of the room. Father would say, "I know you don't like your lessons, but you have to study. Otherwise, you'll amount to nothing; people will make fun of you. We love you and we want everyone to respect you." . . . And in the morning, when Sara again did not wake up on time, Father slapped her with his heavy hand. Mother said, "Dorna, at school, tell them you ran into a door." But Sara told everyone what had happened, and she didn't say why.

"We're getting tired," Father said now. "Let's take a taxi."

Father didn't know the name of the street where the cemetery was. Every now and then when a taxi drove by, he leaned forward and shouted, "Cemetery?"

The cemetery was on a crowded street with plenty of trees. There were soldiers. There were flags. Dorna counted the coffins: eleven ... The soldiers sang an anthem.

"They're the martyrs of war," Father said, pointing at the coffins.

And he turned away. Dorna knew he wanted to cry. She asked, "Then why doesn't Sara have a coffin?"

"How do you know what a coffin is?" Father asked.

Dorna counted the coffins: twelve ...

Father said, "You have to stay right here and wait until I come back. Don't wander off; you'll get lost." And he left. Dorna looked at the women wearing black chadors and crying. She didn't like black chadors. She looked at the framed photographs in front of the coffins. The photographs looked back at her. She saw fragments of the sun; they were bubbling, simmering, the color of the delicious quince jam that Mother made, that Sara didn't like. The green shadows of the trees were everywhere, and in between everywhere, here and there, there were patches of sun. As people walked by, the patches jumped up on them and then fell down on the ground again. The men beat their chests and mourned. They looked like they were grabbing something from the air above their heads and beating it against their chests. Through the fence, Dorna peeked in at the cemetery. For one second, she thought she saw Father nearby, and then the people coming and going blocked her view. She wanted to go to the end of the street. She looked up. She could see pieces of the sky between the leaves. Blue and green, the blue had an end and the white cloud was no longer there. She wanted to go to the end of the street. One day, once upon a time, they had left the bicycle in the alley and wandered off. Dorna had said, "Let's go." And they'd followed the hunchback with a cane. The old man walked slowly. They hunched their backs, just like he did, and dragged their heels as they went. The old man found a human eye. He put it in his pocket. His jacket pockets were down by his knees.

Father came back. "Let's go."

"But why didn't Sara have a coffin?"

"Little children don't need coffins. They jump straight to heaven."

"They jump from where?"

"From here."

The old hunchback was walking with his cane ahead of them. He saw a pair of fingers on the sidewalk. He went to pick them up. He bent down like children who fold at the waist and touch their heads to the ground. Across the street, next to a lot of gravestones, a man was kneeling on the ground, hitting a chisel against a slab of stone.

Father said, "I saw Sara go up to the sky. Now, you're alone; you're by yourself. Maybe when the war is over, Mother will bring a brother or sister for you. Then you'll be together; you won't be alone anymore."

Father rubbed his hands together. The old man was still up ahead. He walked along without hearing them. He patiently walked, just as he always walked. . . . That bicycle day, that once-upon-a-time day, when they went back home, there was no one there and it was dark. Then Father and Mother came. Mother cried and Father just stared. They had brought the bicycle in from the alley. Father angrily said that they had searched everywhere and told all the policemen, and then he sat down and said, "I know it's all Sara's fault. She tricked you to . . ." Dorna said, "No. I tricked her." But Father didn't believe her. . . . The old man bent down and picked up a marble and put it in his pocket. Father was looking up at the sky. Suddenly, he stopped.

"Do you hear a siren?"

"No."

When they arrived home, Mother had cooked Dorna's favorite dish. Father didn't eat lunch. He went and sat on the easy chair where he always sat and he smoked a cigarette. After lunch, Dorna went to her room. The walls were covered with Sara's handwriting: *One day a sparrow . . . divisions are stupid . . . drawings like to play* . . . Dorna had asked Sara, "Which do you like more, additions or subtractions?" . . . *Rain falls on the . . . Death to stupid, wicked Soleimanzadeh* . . . Sara had grabbed at Soleimanzadeh's Islamic headdress and pulled her hair. The school principal had told Mother, "Madam, if tomorrow this wild girl stabs a student in the eye with a pen, who is answerable?" Sara had shouted, "Soleiman-zadeh took my friend to play a game and she wouldn't let me play with them." The principal had said, "You are a liar." Sara had screamed, "You bitch! . . . You bitch! . . ." And she had run out into the schoolyard, shrieking, "Aaa—a! . . ." Snaking squiggles in red on the back of the door . . . *crows . . . lots of crows* . . . from the closet all the way to the window . . . *let's go play . . . death to . . .*

And Sara was no longer there. From her room, Dorna called out, "Can I go out to the yard?"

"Sit down and draw a few pictures!"

"But school is closed."

"The hell with school. You sit down and draw. . . . For just one hour, sit still and do something."

From the window, she could see the petals of sour orange blossoms falling one by one. They fluttered gently, like feathers, like snowflakes. . . . She could smell Father's cigarette. The radio was on, so that they would know when the red-alert sirens went off, so that they could run and huddle under the stairs.

Mother said, "Let's go away somewhere."

"Where is there for us to go?" Father replied.

"The upstairs neighbors left this morning."

They sounded like they had made up.

"Where can we go that won't be like this? Be patient."

Father walked into her room.

"Why are you crying, my girl?"

"It's nothing."

"You're crying over nothing?"

Father paused and then asked again, "Why are you crying?"

"The teacher said whoever is bad will go to hell. You sent Sara to hell."

"No, my girl. For Sara . . . You need to understand this. For Sara, it's much better this way. Now, you . . ." And he walked out, and Dorna closed her eyes.

Mother said, "Now, do you understand what you've done by fabricating that Sara for her? You maniac!"

"Stop it! She'll forget in a day or two. You don't understand . . . you don't understand anything. What else could I have done?"

And their voices drifted away and the sour oranges turned the color of shadows. Then there was the sound of Father sobbing out in the yard, and the dark grew thicker, and like winter nights when she buried her head under the down blanket and it grew warm, the dark grew warm, and she woke up, realizing she was sleeping on the floor, and she didn't remember when the sheet had been draped over her. She thought hard, but she didn't know whether it was yesterday, today, or tomorrow, and it was night and the light in her room was turned off, and there was a rustle behind the window. Quietly, she said, "Sara? . . ."

And she heard, "Shhh! . . . What do you want?"

"I brought this for you from near the cemetery." And she opened her fist, clenched since morning and full of the perfume of sour orange blossoms, for Sara.

King of the Graveyard

Dedicated to Iran's forbidden graves

FROM THE FOOT OF THE WALL of the fifth ruin, nine steps toward the ash tree, then seven steps to the right.

I say, "Marokh Khanoom!* It's not just your son's grave; he was my son, too. I'm sure it was right here. And this thornbush that you say wasn't here before, you're absolutely right. It grew since the last time we came."

Well, it's difficult. In a sprawling wasteland, how is one to remember where one's child is buried?

I say, "Trust this old man. I know this graveyard like the back of my hand. Test me if you have any doubts. For instance, if we enter the graveyard from these ruins, if we take this straight path, we'll be in section three twenty-seven. The first grave with the two stone candelabras belongs to Mr. Semiromi—the family elder who passed away in 1973. Bibi Khatoon, that kind and hardworking mother, is resting on the other side. Next is Mr. Yadi's grave, so innocent . . . If we keep going straight, we'll reach a marble gravestone; it comes up to my knees, really beautiful and fitting:

---

* *Khanoom* means lady, madam, or missus.

Kazem Khan Rabandi, high-ranking retiree of the Department of Education. . . . Shall I go on? I swear I know the next section like the back of my hand, too. So believe me when I tell you that it was this exact spot that I measured in steps last month."

And every Friday night, Mahrokh Khanoom starts nagging like a broken record. She insists and insists and again I have to make her understand: Madam! We don't have a choice! For them not to grow suspicious, we shouldn't go to the cemetery that often. In fact, each time we have to wait more than a month before going there again. And whenever we go, we have to stop by other places, as well. She starts to weep.

I say, "Madam, we were at the cemetery just last week."

She says, "Sir! You're forgetful and absentminded. It's been more than a month. I dare you to tell me what day of the week this is."

I say, "But the X that you scratched on the dirt wasn't much of a marker. Did you really expect it to stay there for a month?"

She says, "It's all the Hemmatis' doing. They're thirsty for our blood—mine and yours, old man. Why do you harass us? You're my man; where's your sense of honor? Go over there and tell them that it doesn't please God when they torment a bereaved old woman like this. Show some backbone and ask them, 'What do you have to lose if we put a rock or a marker here?' Why won't it at least rain?"

I say, "Rest assured, it was right here. Cover your

face with your chador so that if someone sees you, they won't notice you're crying. Let them think we've given up searching and searching again and are just sitting here for no reason."

I say, "And tonight we, too, will go and break their son's marble stone."

Mahrokh Khanoom frowns. She says, "No! I'll go tell them myself."

She rushes off irately. Panting, I run after her. I shout, "Mahrokh Khanoom, come back! Leave them alone. They'll ruin us."

I don't know what stood here before, in this remote corner of the graveyard, all these caved-in mud walls, next to the haven of beautiful and proper graves. All those times, a thousand times, maybe more, when despite the frailty of old age I searched the graveyard, I never suspected these ruins. Perhaps some fifty years ago these walls were the homes of God's sheep. These openings were perhaps windows. In springtime, people would look out from them. Perhaps someone had a sweetheart, and this very wall that is our marker might have been a room; in it he had kissed and held his darling. . . . And then the cemetery quickly spread and pressed forward until it reached here. . . . The drawn-out revolution, the dragged-out war.

I say, "A cemetery should be sacred and have boundaries; its residents should have their own proper stones, name and identity. . . . When there are no gravestones, when a Quran reader refuses to come here even if you pay him a hundred thousand tomans, then what is this place? Then who are we, Mahrokh Khanoom?"

I don't know, I don't remember in which wall in the basement I hid my father's revolver. It was perhaps forty, fifty years ago that I hid it there. I will find it, even if I have to break every wall.

I say, "Mahrokh Khanoom, have no qualms. I remember exactly. Piriza told me to measure in steps from the wall. First, seven steps, then nine steps."

She says, "The moment I touch the earth, I know in my heart whether my child is buried in it or not. Believe me when I tell you he's not here. Sir, your memory has gotten a bit muddled. If you're right, tell me if it is now, yesterday, or today. . . . Where are the seven stones that I stacked on top of one another as a marker?"

I say, "Stones can't serve as a marker. It's like telling someone that our house is the one with a pigeon sitting on the edge of its roof. Perhaps a kid picked up the stones and hurled them at a sparrow, a cat, or something."

She says, "Children don't come here. And of all the sparrows here, have you ever heard one of them chirp?"

I haven't. . . . But from someplace far away, distant voices constantly call my name: "Heydar, Heydar! Put on your shoes." . . . Sometimes it seems the things I remember belong to another man's life, a life that I have only witnessed: My Mahrokh, sitting beside the window with the pure sun shining on her plump and ample calves, with one end of a thread tied around her big toe and the other end wrapped around her fingers, she rolls the thread's weave above her upper lip, sparse strands of hair get caught and are plucked out, and my Mahrokh's face glistens like marble.

I say, "My mate! At home, there's nothing to fear. Weep and wail as much as you want. If you don't want to cry, at least talk, reminisce. The way you stare blankly at these walls, with each month that passes you age a year. Where is my sweet sugar candy?"

Mahrokh, the hem of her chador rustling on the ground, moves from one ruin to the next, and to the one after that, hoping that something will seem familiar to her. I think my old woman's memory has become muddled.

She says, "The ruins have all become identical. It's the Hemmatis' doing. You're just playing dumb. Right now, that husband and wife are somewhere watching us, laughing at how we wander around, lost and confused. How much food do these people stuff themselves with that they can dump their dung all around here? There must be other children's graves here, too. We must tell their mothers."

I say, "My good woman, that's all we need—for them to arrest us for exposing secret government information."

I've never seen the Hemmatis laugh. I've never come to the cemetery and not found them at their son's grave. They're always dressed in black. Sitting there, they look like they've turned into stone. But one of these days, there will be an opportunity for my plan

and I will take my revenge on that one-armed Hemmati. If I corner him in a dark and secluded place, this
rage that I have will put strength in my arms. With his
white hair and beard, he's about the same age as me, but
he looks so sickly that I'm sure he's no match for me. It's
not that I'm afraid of that piercing look in his eyes, but
in his gaze I see old hatred. Perhaps over the years the
husband and wife have fed and fattened it and they've
plotted to avenge their son's blood.

I don't remember when I said it, but I once said,
"You're our savior, Mr. Piriza! I searched the entire
cemetery. I peeked into every nook and cranny. I cozied
up to anyone just so that I could get the person to
talk, so that I could get some information. Wherever
I saw a couple of people chatting, I moved up close so
that I could hear what they were saying. Whenever I
came across the grave of a youth deprived of life, I sat
and tapped a pebble three times on his headstone and
recited the prayer for the dead. After all, these young
people will see one another in the world beyond and
they will tell one another. Perhaps they will let my son
know that I'm searching for his grave. Was I right, Mr.
Piriza? Maybe it was my son who put the thought in
your head to come and tell me where he is."

Then the wind always blows. In the summer, the
blistering sun scorches the earth. Burned dust gets
into one's throat. Who knows whose dust it is? At least
the martyrs' section is better. They've covered it with
tarpaulin; it's shaded. Whenever I can no longer stand
the heat, I go and sit there. The graves have pictures.

I tell the martyrs of war, "Too bad I wasn't young and couldn't go with you to fight. I have a revolver, from the days of the coup d'état. I've hidden it in a wall in the basement."

I say, "I can't remember if I told you or not. I came face-to-face with Hemmati. It was just yesterday, or the day before. I came face-to-face with Hemmati. He walked straight toward me so that I would have to step aside. I didn't. We ended up face-to-face. He glared at me as if he wanted to sink his teeth into my jugular. Right there. He hollered, 'Move aside!' I said, 'You move aside.' He didn't. He said, 'I told you to step aside.' I said, 'And I told you to step aside.' He leaned toward me like a ram wanting to butt heads. I did the same, just so that our foreheads touched."

How quickly the night comes. I should say, Mahrokh Khanoom, come now, we should go home. Our house is all alone. Let's go.

I must remember that no matter what I say, I should be careful not to mention the nagging suspicion that has crept into my mind. I almost let it slip yesterday. Mahrokh Khanoom won't be able to bear this one. The moment I blurt out the words, she will heave a sigh and surrender her life to the Life-giver.

Walking back in the dark, time passes more quickly. But on the other end, the night drags out. I quietly say, "Madam! May God strike me mute if I cause you to worry, but when we reach the bend in the alley, casually turn and look behind. It seems someone from the adjoining section is shadowing us."

Mahrokh Khanoom turns the key in the lock and opens the front door. In the courtyard, beside this shallow pool empty of fish, I should sit and think about what I ought to do. Should I tell my Mahrokh or not? Well, it's true that ever since I told her I've found our son's grave, she doesn't sit there as silent and still as a corpse, so that I sometimes feared she might be dead. Now my Mahrokh seems to have new life in her. For me to now tell her . . . What was it I wanted to tell her? . . . Old age and darkness, by the time one finishes a thought, the moon has climbed up from behind the courtyard wall. Those days when there were red fish in the pool, they used to play around the moon's reflection on the water; they played so much. But close to dawn, when the earth and sky would grow quiet, when you couldn't even hear the rustle of the leaves on the bitter orange trees, a strange sound of splattering would come from the pool. I knew the fish had swum up and with their lips on the surface of the water they were opening and closing their mouths. They weren't sucking in air; they weren't hungry; they were talking in their own language. Perhaps they were even telling one another that in the morning a Revolutionary Guard would knock on the front door. . . .

Tonight, I will dig out my revolver from the basement wall. It's been sleeping for far too many years. For so long I've been saying, "Mahrokh Khanoom, you're always out shopping; why don't you also buy a pair of goldfish for the shallow pool? It'll be pleasant and cheerful. On late afternoons, it will be fun for me to sit and watch them." She says, "It may bring good fortune or bad fortune to the house." I say, "What good or bad fortune is there left for us, madam?"

My breath, gasping, gasping . . . I gasp; I'm short of breath. I once said, or I will say, "Mahrokh Khanoom, I have good news. Some good soul has come our way who knows where our son is buried."

From the foot of the ruins of the fifth wall, nine steps toward the ash tree. Then seven steps to the . . . Did Piriza say to the right or to the left?

Piriza says, "Phhh! . . . Enough of all this gloating. Your son was no bouquet of roses, nor was he much to brag about. No matter how much you boast that he was an angel from heaven, I, for one, won't believe that he was falsely accused. Here, they call me King of the Graveyard. I know every nitty-gritty detail about the residents."

I say, "Then you should know better than anyone that my son was unjustly accused. That morning my son was on his way to work. He was minding his own business. They had just hired him at the Beacon of Wisdom bookstore. He would have had a good future if—"

"Khe khe . . ." The way Piriza snickers, he must be mocking me. At least my Mahrokh isn't here to see how contemptuously he laughs at me. He says, "No, chump! Your story is a far cry from theirs. That morning, their son said good-bye and headed for work. Just three or four minutes later, they heard a knock on the door. . . . They confided in me."

"My son didn't know how to shoot a gun at all."

"When they ran to the door, the boy was already on his knees, with his hand still on the knocker, as if it was welded to it. The poor things; at first they had no clue what had happened. From the head of the alley where their son had been hit, they saw blood on the ground for thirty or forty meters, all the way up to their son's knees. It was only then that they saw blood gushing out of his stomach."

I say, "No! As God is my witness, no. . . . It was their son who together with his buddies started chasing my son. What will a nineteen-year-old do when he sees three or four guys with guns chasing after him? My son was running away. They started to shoot. A bullet hit their son."

"That's a tall story, old man. If they get their hands on you, they'll whack off your head and hand it to you. It's old age and senility. What do you know? These people were born with venom in their blood. That one-armed man let me in on it himself. To this day, his wife jolts awake in the middle of the night and screams. She hears knocking on the door. She confided in me that every time she opens the front door, she sees her son drenched in blood, on his knees. . . . I mean, don't count on them forgetting. If you want me to bring them around, it's going to cost you money. You have to cough it up."

For a few years now, a chilling weakness comes over me and suddenly my knees give way. I don't want to fall to my knees in front of Mahrokh Khanoom. But as soon as I sit down, the chill comes. . . . From inside my veins it creeps to my fingertips, like the iciness of snow. The chill is not alive. It's a lifeless cold that at times moves all the way up to my eyes; my eyes water. Icy drops slide down my face.

My vision is blurred. I should say, Madam, casually glance over at the adjacent plot. It seems someone is taking a photograph of us.

I say, "You're going to make me measure this place so many times that everyone will finally suspect we're up to something. Mahrokh Khanoom, let this be the last time. I still hear Piriza's words as clearly as I did on that very first day. He said from the foot of this wall, seven steps to the right, toward the ash tree. . . . Right? Then he said nine steps to the left. . . . Half a step more or less makes no difference."

She says, "No, sir! . . . I'm a mother. Mothers know in their hearts, especially if it has to do with their child. It was somewhere else. There's nothing here under this soil."

It's damn cold. Here the wind always blows; it blows even more in autumn. The ruins' walls, all the same height and size, all looking alike . . . Our marker was perhaps this very wall with the two window holes.

Next time, I'll make a refreshing drink. Have I told Mahrokh Khanoom that I bought cyanide from Piriza? No, I haven't. And I should remember not to. I'm sure Piriza understood what I want it for but paid no mind. If I mix cyanide powder in a refreshing drink, I know how and by whom to deliver it to Hemmati. That person will tell him, "Please take it! It's an offering." After

Hemmati has gulped it down, when his body has completely absorbed it, I'll show up in front of him and say, "Do you know what was in that drink? Enjoy! What harm did it do to you, the four stones that my poor wife would stack up, happy at last that her son's grave is marked? . . . Enjoy! Now go to our son's grave again, but this time crap will come out of your mouth and gut instead of the hole in your rear end."

The goldfish in the shallow pool, free from all the malice in the world, were gently swimming. Suddenly they flapped their fins and escaped to the bottom of the pool. Someone was knocking.

I say, "Madam! Don't you want to give us any dinner?"

It seems she can't hear me. She's staring at the empty china bowl next to the samovar and the tea set.

She says, "Have you seen the stone they've set for their son? It must be pure marble. It's beautiful. It glows like a mirror when the sun shines on it. For our son, I want . . ."

The floral china bowl . . . It's been years since Mahrokh Khanoom seeded pomegranates and brought them for me in a china bowl with red flowers on it. If she does this, it will be healing for bile and gall.

But for the hundredth time she says, "Why did you burn everything that was a reminder of my son? If I had his picture, his book, I would be happy with them. I would smell his undershirts; he would come alive in my heart. All this useless fear and caution. You have a heart of stone."

114 Seasons of Purgatory

I know if I try to stand, my knees will give way and I will fall. I sit. . . . Those days when we were never bored and people came and went in our house, our pool was filled with goldfish. Now, no living soul comes to our home.

I say, "Well, when they don't come to our home, it means they don't want to socialize with us. Just like my cousin and the others. Like Haaj Agha, your upstanding brother. Perhaps people are scared of mingling with the parents of an antirevolutionary."

I say, "Do you remember the day I came home and told you that by chance I had wound up at the cemetery and found a guy called Piriza? How could I have promised him money when I knew we didn't have any? What if this guy took our money and just fed us a bunch of lies?"

She says, "You've just come to think of this now, after all this time? I've forgiven him. I always say a prayer for him just for having told us where our son's grave is. Even if he had asked for more, I would have sold the copper pot and tray from my dowry and paid him. What's more, he said he would spend the money on charitable deeds. He'd pay for people to pray and fast. This shows that he's a pious man. In these times of impostors and charlatans, he knows what's religiously sanctioned and what's not."

In these times, the days pass so slowly. When I open my eyes in the morning, my vision is blurred. It's as if there are clouds everywhere. Then I remember that there is a dread in my heart that frightens me. What do women know? They don't know that sometimes there is a fear in a man's heart that he has neither the guts to speak of nor the tolerance to keep to himself.

His face like the wrinkled face of a newborn, his skin the color of camphor, Piriza had said, "Hey, chump! Don't play dumb with me. You should've brought the thirty thousand tomans, the balance due we agreed on. Do you get how dangerous it was for me to let slip where your son is? No! You don't get anything. Old age and senility. If you don't bring the money by the end of the week, I'll make sure they bury you and your old woman right next to your Communist son."

The wind has brought dry leaves and piled them up beside the graves, and the wind brings new leaves.

I say, "Damn! . . . Look, madam. Last time we came, I secretly marked an X at the foot of the wall that was our marker. Now look, they've put an X on all the walls."

Mahrokh Khanoom growls, "You're supposed to be our man, this boy's and mine. Aren't you going to say something to them?"

I say, "No. We shouldn't show our hand. Tonight, after they leave, we'll go and break their son's marble stone."

Mahrokh Khanoom is incensed. "No! I will go and tell them myself."

She wraps her chador around her and heads toward the Hemmatis. My heart is bursting.

I shout, "Mahrokh Khanoom! For the love of God . . . Don't ruin us! Madam! Come back!"

And one sunset, Mahrokh Khanoom screamed in the middle of the courtyard, "I swear to this sunset, oh God, bring misery to those who slaughter people's tattered hearts." And I shouted, "Madam, don't scream! The neighbors, the Hemmatis a few doors away, they will hear and report us."

Now it doesn't seem as if there was ever any voice other than mine and Mahrokh's in this house. The thought of it makes me sad. It was because of this sorrow that I would go out pretending that I wanted to go look at the still shots of the movies posted outside the cinema, and I would instead go to the cemetery and search. In the years I've spent searching, the number of deaths has increased. They bring new corpses all the time. I tell the Afghani boys who wash gravestones, "In the old days, a year would roll by until another person died, a stranger, an unknown. In recent years, twenty-year-old boys keep dying of heart attacks. Stalwart men die of sorrow, like Mr. Yadi."

Suspicious, she would always ask, "Where were you?" And I would say, "I went to see the photos outside the cinema."

Then one day I said, "Mahrokh Khanoom, after all these years, today I went by the cemetery. There's a group of Afghani boys there. It seems they take the flowers that people leave on the graves of their loved ones and give them to a man called Piriza, and he sells them. Don't you think he's forcing them to do this?" She said, "Yes, I've seen them."

She let it slip that she'd seen them. Then she

realized that she had tipped her hand. I learned that she, too . . . So all those times when my Mahrokh said she was going to pray at the shrine of Seyyed Haaj Gharib, she was going to the cemetery, hoping for some information. Perhaps she's been going there for several years. Perhaps the few times I thought I saw someone who looked like Mahrokh wrapped in a chador, it was, in fact, her.

She has persistently said, "You have a heart of stone. I want to light a candle on his grave. I've made a vow to God. Why won't you let me light a candle? Just one. Nothing good will come of my not fulfilling my vow."

And I have repeatedly said, "Mahrokh Khanoom, when do you want to finally stop wearing black?"

And still, still, she's heading recklessly toward the Hemmatis. No matter how hard I try, I can't catch up with her. I shout, "Mahrokh Khanoom! It's going to end in bloodshed!" My steps are weak. . . . By the time I reach her, Mahrokh is sitting next to that woman. She has put her finger on the grave of their son and she's reciting a prayer for the dead. She sounds different. The husband and wife have turned away from her, as if my Mahrokh isn't sitting right next to them. Mahrokh Khanoom finds the woman's hand under her chador and clasps it in her hands.

"It wasn't my son. I swear to the honor of the Prophet's daughter, Zahra, that he was falsely accused."

The woman ignores her. Mahrokh Khanoom, my proud Mahrokh, she pleads, "But whatever it was, whatever happened, he paid the price. . . . We paid the

price, too. Absolve me . . . show forbearance, munifi-
cence. In God's name, forgive him."

The woman glances at her man. Hemmati shakes
his head. Mahrokh has belittled herself. The woman
bends down and rests her forehead on the gravestone.
The man has folded up his left sleeve and pinned it to
the shoulder of his jacket. He shoves his other hand in
his pocket. . . . Perhaps he has a gun.

I say, "Let's go, Mahrokh Khanoom. This isn't the
time and day for this."

I say, "Remember, Mahrokh Khanoom! By Piriza's
account, from the foot of this wall seven steps . . ."

Mahrokh says, "When the earth is laden, it somehow shows it. I just want to sit at my son's grave to my
heart's content, light a candle for him, pour my heart
out to him. There's so much I want to say; all that has
remained unsaid for seven, eight years."

These days, I'm afraid that perhaps some things
have switched places and I don't remember. . . . But
Mahrokh Khanoom shouldn't be throwing it in my
face all the time that I've become forgetful. How come
I still remember the first time my hand touched hers?
One night when Mahrokh is in the right mood, I will
say, "Do you remember that day when I was thirsty?
Remember, it was summertime." And I remember my
hand trembling toward hers. Mahrokh's hand, the
beautiful dimples on her knuckles, her soft skin in that
blazing summer. She held a crystal glass filled to the
rim with water, the reflection of the green leaves of the

bitter orange tree on it, her fingers around the glass, and I slid my fingers in between hers. The young girl's hand trembled. Water spilled. Our hands wet, together. And I said, "Mahrokh, will you be my wife?"

Piriza growls in my face, "Hey, chump! Are you dense? I keep telling you to be discreet, but it doesn't sink into your head. If they figure out that you've found him, they'll dig up his rotting remains and bury them someplace else."

I say, "Madam! Earth to earth is connected. Down there, they hear our footsteps when we come, they hear our footsteps when we leave. We don't have to be right over his head."

She says, "Help me clean up all this trash and scum they've scattered around here. This time, I brought a bag."

I say, "Did you see the Hemmatis? Their son's gravestone is all shattered. It's their penance; perhaps even the broken pieces are lost. I reveled in the moment."

She says nothing.

And she squats down. She's become such an expert. Her chador draped over her head, she skillfully pulls its two sides together like a tent. Even if someone were to pay close attention, they wouldn't realize. Only I know that under her chador she is now unscrewing the top of a bottle of rose water. The scent of rose water, the scent of sun-beaten thirsty earth . . . A distant voice calls out, "Heydar! Heydar! Put on your shoes; I want to take you to Shahrdari circle; they're . . ."

And I have seen Mahrokh's smile ever since Piriza

showed us where our son is. I say, "Those days when you secretly went to the cemetery to make inquiries, you probably saw me there."

She says, "Of course I did. After all these years, do you expect me not to know when you're lying to me?"

"All those times I lied and said I was going to look at the photos outside the cinema, you should have at least confronted me, so that lying wouldn't be counted among my wrongdoings. I swear to God, the sin of all these lies is on your shoulders."

I like it when she smiles like this. In the old days, when she had the heart and spirit, sweet, how sweet and pretty, and I would instantly want her.

Now, shrouded by her chador, Mahrokh Khanoom is talking to our son. "You father wasn't feeling well. All night, in the cold, he stood guard over you. He thinks he still has some youth left in him. I died a thousand deaths until his fever broke. . . . Soften up Heydar's heart so he'll let me light a candle on your grave. I've walked around the shrine of Seyyed Haaj Gharib and made vows."

And I don't say, Mahrokh Khanoom, there's something in my heart, like a secret, that I don't have the courage to tell you. I'm afraid that again you'll sit in a daze and mutely stare at some distant point.

On the way back, as we walk past the martyrs' section, Hemmati and his wife are still sitting there. They've lit candles on the broken pieces of the gravestone. Seven of them.

The husband's and wife's eyes gleam in the

candlelight. Piriza was right. It's the gleam of hatred and revenge.

I say, "Madam! No matter how hard I think, I don't remember coming here and breaking their gravestone. Did I? When?"

Mahrokh says nothing. Back home, she brings me tea in a small narrow-waisted tea glass. I look out the window; a parrot is sitting at the edge of the shallow pool, dipping its beak in the water and raising its head for the water to flow down its throat.

Mahrokh Khanoom says, "What is troubling you? These days you are often deep in thought."

I say, "I'm thinking of that bangle you sold so that we could pay Piriza. Why was I never able to bring enough money home for my wife and child? . . . For our son, whom we sent to school in the winter wearing only a single layer of clothes. He must have been very cold."

The plaster on the basement wall seems to have frozen, too. It doesn't come off easily. . . . What if Mahrokh Khanoom wakes up and panics? I have to scrape away the mud and straw beneath the plaster with my fingernails. My hand touches the wrapper. . . . I tear away at the seven layers of wrapping. I take out the German revolver. It still smells of the grease I had rubbed on it. I open the cylinder. Four bullets remain inside. . . . When I catch him in a secluded place, I will shout, "Hands up!" He'll raise the one arm he has, and then I'll shoot. I'll empty all four bullets into his hateful heart.

And if there are goldfish in the shallow pool, they will gently swim together, at times their bodies rubbing against one another's. Clearly they like it; they don't quickly pull away. My Mahrokh is sleeping so very deeply. Now I will go back to the cemetery to hunt.

And now the chill of midnight reaches the coldness of my bones. I crouch down behind a ruin wall to lessen the onslaught of the graveyard wind. . . . Even if I'm to freeze, I will sit here until I catch that one-armed Hemmati. Just as he's pulling down his pants to spread his crap all over the place, I will come out from behind the wall and shout, "Do you think God can't see you?" And then I'll empty the bullets. Tomorrow morning when they find him with his pants down, he'll have no honor left.

The shadows have one by one risen from the earth, here and there. . . . Aha! It's him. He's coming. . . . Suddenly, Piriza grabs me.

"What are you doing here at this hour of the night, deadbeat? . . . Getting bold and brash? Are you spying on me, you scoundrel?"

The smell of his breath in my face . . .

"No, Mr. Piriza. It's just a blunder. I fell asleep. I didn't realize I had fallen asleep."

He pounds his fist on my chest. I don't want to fall at his feet. . . . I fall.

"You're all cut from the same cloth. You and your hussy, Hemmati and his wench. The hell with all of you."

In the dark, his figure all a shadow, Piriza walks

away among the graves. He kicks the gravestones as he goes. It's all darkness now.

Mahrokh says, "Dear God, let it rain tomorrow, too. Let it pour from the heavens and skies."

I don't understand why she prays for rain. . . . And it rains all night long. Until the late hours of the night, we silently sit huddled next to the kerosene heater, coupon-bought government-subsidized kerosene, the wick turned low. How pleasant, the sound of rain in the gutters is so pleasant. It doesn't allow you to hear the knock on the door when they come to congratulate you. "Your godless son was executed. We did away with his filthy corpse, less trouble for you. But you have to pay for the bullet." . . . Thank God we didn't have a daughter.

I say, "Mahrokh Khanoom, thank God we didn't have a daughter."

She says, "If we did, she, too, would have courage and honor. My son was a man. He wasn't raised a wimp. He wouldn't be bullied."

I say, "If you say this out on the street, you'll be arrested. They'll take you where no one can save you. I'll be devastated, ruined."

"Well, you can come with me. Like the days when you used to take me to the park."

In her sweet smile there's a hint of sarcasm.

But it's fortunate that we didn't have a girl. Otherwise, like Mr. Yadi's daughter, on the night of her execution they would take her virginity so that she wouldn't go to heaven. The next morning the guy would show up at our door with a box of pastries to tell us he was our bridegroom last night. . . . How Mr. Yadi danced in the middle of the alley, shouting, "Hey, neighbors, come on out and have some pastries. My bridegroom is here." He danced and he wept.

In the middle of my dreams, the sky slowly grows light . . . and it is still raining. Now, like the old days, Mahrokh Khanoom has put walnuts on top of the kerosene heater. Roasted walnuts. Their charred skin peels off at the slightest pressure. They taste wonderful with cheese. Too bad I can't eat that many with these dentures. Mahrokh Khanoom is quick with housework; she seems cheerful.

She says, "Let's go to the cemetery soon."

I don't know why she's happy.

The cemetery is empty. Here and there, a few women wearing black chadors are hunched over gravestones. The walkways are empty. The peddlers, the Afghani boys, they're not here. . . . But Hemmati and his wife are.

I spit at my incompetent self for failing. For failing to catch Hemmati. Now, but now, it's good that the wind is blowing. When the wind beats the raindrops against your face, no one can tell that these are the tears of a man.

Mahrokh Khanoom says, "The good thing about rainy days is that it's quiet here."

The mud walls are wet halfway up from the ground. One of these days what's left of them will collapse. . . . Nine steps . . . Then? . . . Seven steps . . . No matter what I say, Mahrokh won't take the umbrella. My fingertips, cold and wet, in the mud, I pick up onion skins, cigarette butts, empty cans of beans, dried-up crap.

And now that it's again now, I have to walk away to the edge of the pathway and sit there with my back to her and to our son so that no one will grow suspicious.

Later, somehow, in some way that won't break Mahrokh's heart, I have to tell her about the misgiving that has come to me again, that clings to me like a leech, that sucks my will to tell her, that stings and sucks my blood to tell her what if Piriza lied that our son's grave is here. . . .

Once in a while, a few drops of rain fall on my head through the hole in the umbrella. Mahrokh wanted it to rain so that the cemetery would be empty. What if she's planning . . . Panicked, I turn around and look. . . . I force myself to keep my voice down.

"What the hell? Madam, what are you doing?" I shout, "Madam, have you gone mad? Put it out!"

The wind steals the umbrella from my hand. I rush over to her. She ignores me. She's holding one hand to block the wind, the other as a roof over the candle. No matter what I say, she pays no attention to me.

I want to blow out the candle. She raises her head. Her face is all wet; there's a glint and pleading in her eyes. I don't know if the glint in her eyes is from a tear, from joy, or . . . Her lips are trembling.

"I beg you, pl . . . please don't put it out. I've prayed and made a vow."

The wind is taking away my umbrella, black,

rolling away amid the graves. My clothes and body feel heavy, my knees buckle, and I fall down next to Mahrokh. One hand still shielding the candle, the other gently sweeping the rain and pebbles off our son's grave. It looks as if she's caressing the dirt. The flame of the half-burned candle drags in the wind. . . . I don't dare turn and look behind. Perhaps it's one of those shadows I imagine, or perhaps someone is really spying on us. Oh foolish woman! . . . My hand cold and wet, I press it down on the candle. It sinks into the dirt. Mahrokh weeps and whimpers.

"Madam, you've ruined us. Why did you do this?"

With her lips pursed tight, she cries. For the first time in my life, I wish Mahrokh didn't exist, that she was dead, that she never existed to . . . I say, "Now that you've done this, let me tell you and put both our minds at rest. I've had this suspicion for a long time. That bastard Piriza is a swindler. He lied to us."

Stunned, her wails stifled, she says nothing.

I say, "You simpleminded woman, there's no one buried here."

Her look makes me uneasy. . . . I can't bear to see her like this. I should walk away, go stand in the shelter of the ruin walls. The rain has stopped.

I say, "I mean . . . Now . . . Well, we shouldn't have been quick to believe him. I didn't mean to upset you. May God strike me mute."

Mahrokh is no longer shaking her head, nor is she crying through her pursed lips. I can't bear to look at her. It's not raining. It's her voice pouring down.

When did she come behind the ruin wall? I sit on my heels at the foot of the wall. I want to die right here so that I won't feel so damn cold. Dead and distant sounds are coming. They come cold; they come with the wind. . . . A distant voice, farther away than years and years: "Heydar, put on your shoes. I want to take you to Shahrdari circle to look around. . . . They're hanging someone there."

Now, I don't know how much time has passed. My eyes were closed. The voices were taking me with them in the wind while I slept. . . . From far away, Mahrokh's voice . . . She sounds like she does when she wakes me up in the morning. . . . I hope it's still morning, we still haven't come here, I still haven't broken her heart. Mahrokh's voice moves closer. . . . She says, "I know it in my heart. . . . He's right here." She laughs.

I snap out of the numbness of cold.

The one-armed man is standing a short distance away on the walkway. He's glaring at me. . . . I want to say, Mahrokh Khanoom, now do you see? They've come. They've reported us and are waiting for the others to come and take us into custody. But the black swell of Mahrokh's chador isn't alone. Two wet chadors stuck together. Hemmati's wife is sitting next to Mahrokh. Sitting, she's planting a candle in the earth. Then Mahrokh, too, lights one.

ooooo

I say, "Mahrokh Khanoom, after all, a man, too, sometimes has a fear, a suspicion in his heart. . . . Forgive me. I think even if I wanted to shoot those four bullets, they wouldn't fire. After all these years, the gunpowder must be damp. . . . Well, you're right. You're right, rainwater has washed away the drops of wax and the ends of the candles . . ."

"So then, from the foot of this wall I have to count seven steps toward the ash tree. . . . Right? . . . Then nine steps to the left . . ."

The Color of Midday Fire

DARKNESS ... DARKNESS ... how mysterious it is. Man is at a loss for what to do. But it is clear that man is of one species and leopard is of another. If in close proximity, it is inevitable for them to come face-to-face, and then they must fight until only one walks away and the other remains on the ground—the earth's share, or that of the vultures and hyenas that on such occasions are undoubtedly nearby. It is because of such thoughts that I wanted to escape the city. When I returned from exile overseas, I came directly here. From the estates of a rural landowner, regardless of how much is taken away by land reform and the revolution, enough remains for his grandchild's morning milk and evening meat and for cartridges for his hunting rifle. Enough remains for me to live this life of tribal enmities to its end. This is what I had planned, but one never knows what tomorrow may bring. How could I have known that this tranquility would be disrupted and that I would find myself standing between man and leopard? And how I hate being caught in the middle. . . . Look at this fire that I specifically asked them to light for you! It is the color of blood. Because in this, too, there is the temptation to fight. I was saying . . .

I told Captain Meena, just as I'm telling you now, that the harsh nature of our region is no longer suitable

for him. He was a tough man; he wouldn't listen to anyone. With his cold eyes, he would glare at people as if
he were considering how to break their necks if they
were to come to blows. But you are well educated and
you understand what I mean. I told the captain it would
be best if he went to the Caspian coast up north to rest
and to forget. The nature there is gentle and forgiving,
like the flight of a sea swallow above the line where
water and shore meet, or like the stillness of the fog
that lingers above the forests. He didn't agree.

I was in his debt. We first met years ago, when
he was an unknown lieutenant in a small garrison in
our province. Unlike now, I was a restless young man.
On a few occasions he released my hunting rifles after
they were confiscated by the gamekeepers. From then
on, together we would sneak into the royal hunting
grounds and hunt. It was with me that he first tasted
the still-pulsating liver of a deer. I taught him to hold
the warm liver against a hot stone by the fire and to
sink his teeth into it while it still had blood. In the
course of these pastimes, our acquaintance evolved
into a friendship. That's why when he came with his
wife and three-year-old daughter to spend his sick
leave here, I welcomed him.

Six years of war had worn him out. He had a certain
nervous and harried behavior. He said he didn't want
such shame and dishonor but that the brigade doctor
had prescribed a compulsory one-month leave. I said,
"It's a sign of old age, after all." He slammed his fist
against this very wall and said, "No." The plaster still

bears the imprint of his knuckle. Look . . . And he used to take pills that, regardless of what they were, didn't agree with the temperament of an officer in an airborne commando brigade. A man's pill is his heart—he gnaws at it and calms down. The morning of the second day, he held his daughter in his arms, went and sat under the eucalyptus tree in the garden, and listened to her chatter, like a patient nursemaid. I went and sat with them. The little girl was talking about a doll that woke up in the middle of the night and fussed for her father. She was sweet. I said, "My friend, let's go for a ride." He was captivated by the child. He had been wounded a few times by mortar shrapnel, and after two or three surgeries a few pieces still remained lodged near his vertebrae. He would sit up straight, with his eyes in a fixed gaze. Unlike me, he had developed neither a large stomach nor a kidney stone, but the hair on his temples had turned gray. . . . Have some of this kebab. . . . I don't eat much. I don't want to gain weight. My blood must remain thin and I have to stay agile.

The captain's wife spoke little. She was one of those women who hear sounds from the future, and they wait, and they don't reveal their fears and anxieties. She didn't like it here at all. But she was so fed up with the captain's lengthy missions that she didn't complain at all. The little girl, either. Ever since she was born, her father had been at the front. She would cling to the captain and caress his unshaven face. Captain Meena would bite her. He would bite the girl's plump arms, her lips, her chubby hands. . . . Don't let this fire burn in vain. Skewer some meat. Fire will turn to ashes. . . .

The first night the captain and I were alone together, we sat on the rooftop and started regurgitating memories of our youth. The pleasant scent of freshly harvested alfalfa and wild mint makes one want to talk. Of course, only if there's no smell of peasants. . . . Even peasants who have turned into landowners still have that old smell. Once, only once, did the captain and I feel helpless before the gaze of a wounded deer. His spine had broken from the bullet's impact; he was dragging his paralyzed hind legs on the ground. When we reached him, he stood completely still. It was near dusk; in his eyes there was neither fear nor a plea for mercy. Truth be told, we froze. I wouldn't say the deer's gaze frightened us. What we felt was fear, but it wasn't just fear. It was remorse, and it wasn't just remorse. But finally Captain Meena slashed the deer's jugular with his serrated knife. After all, he didn't believe jinns in deerskin wander around the prairies. That night, on the rooftop, we recalled that we hadn't eaten that deer's liver. And we couldn't remember having eaten its flesh, either. It seems we gave it away. Then the captain lay down and folded his hands under his head and gazed up at the stars. Our region has a sky full of shooting stars, because it has many devils, too. I was starting to get bored when he began sharing his memories of war. I thought to myself, Let him talk, let him get it off his chest.

During the war, he led a commando unit. A sharp-shooter . . . His stories made me forget sleep. I have childhood memories of tribal gunfights. The blood of one or two people would be shed, and the day after the skirmish, time and life, homes and farms, all would all be as they had been before. Not like the war the captain talked about. My imagination could not stretch to the devastation a booby trap wreaks on the legs, arms, chest, and head of a commando. Near dawn, the captain jolted from his sleep, shouting. He had dreamed of a few boots that had been thrown into the air and were gently twirling down. They fell to the ground. Their laces had been carefully tied into a bow. Blood was gushing from between the laces. The boots weren't empty; legs severed mid-calf remained in them. . . . I gave him some water and put him back to sleep, but up until sunrise there were beads of sweat on his forehead and he was panting. I was now certain that it was my responsibility to take care of him. But he was restless and soon turned bitter and belligerent. Just like the times when we were young, I organized a shooting match. In those days, we used to brag and boast to each other a lot. His constantly shaking hands quieted down when he held the Brno rifle. His eyes gleamed. He inspected it and said, "Compared to the latest rifles, it looks like a bludgeon. Pulling the breechblock one shot at a time, what's the point? With today's rifles, one squeeze of the trigger makes a colander out of the other guy." I said, "Brno is a man's rifle; you have one chance at the shot." He snickered and handed the rifle back to me. He said, "Let me see you take the shot." I didn't hit the target. Nowadays, when a five rial coin is too far away, I see only a vague blur. I said, "Old-age fat has reached my eyes." He was excited. His little girl was clapping for him. His wife had covered her ears. He aimed. He gently half-cocked the hammer. He held his breath. It was as if he were sitting in ambush behind a rock and aiming at someone's heart. He pulled the trigger. He gave the rifle back to me and said, "Even without fat, you were no match for me." His wife clapped for him, which I didn't quite appreciate, and the girl leaped into his arms. . . .

Are you tired? . . . Listen! . . . The mountain is not close by, but the wind carries sounds. Sometimes it's a woman's wail, sometimes a man's howl, sometimes a leopard's roar. . . . Don't be impatient; once I explain the entire incident, you will get to know one of this world's greatest darknesses. . . . On the fourth or fifth day of their stay, we went to the waterfall. There is no sound but the sound of water there. The captain's little girl was excited. We spread our gear under an oak tree beside the stream and stretched out. The scent of wild mint and the water's mist were intoxicating. The woman fell asleep at her husband's feet. The little girl was running back and forth along the stream, chasing dragonflies. The same blue-and-purple dragonflies that we see, and it's hard to believe that they might bear the seeds of death. The captain and I, facing the waterfall, with one eye on the rainbow across the fall and the other on each other, were talking about the differences between youth and middle age. Just like now, I was feeling chatty. At one point I turned and saw the little girl holding out her arms and chasing a dragonfly along the stream. I'll never forget how her shiny chestnut hair was waving in the air. The captain was talking about ambushes along the route of moving enemy columns. In a narrow canyon, they hit the first and last vehicles with RPG-7s and trapped the others in between. Shadows leaped out of the vehicles, and they, up on an elevation, in the glow of the flames, took their time and immobilized every single one of them. The captain used to say that in battle, the most important thing is not to be caught off guard. But sir, nature uses these moments of inattention as a means of self-preservation. The wind, in an instant of the earth's inattention, casts a seed in a crevice; the birds are neglectful of the seed and it grows. Sir, the pollen reaches a pistil when bees and butterflies are neglectful. In a hunter's heedlessness, the wild goat appears to be a rock or tumbleweed. . . . I was going to suggest to the captain that after his wife woke up we take a walk up to the top of the waterfall and come straight back so that he would see which one of us had been impaired by age, but just then, I heard that scream. It was brief. It sounded as if the little girl had fallen down or a thorn had pricked her leg. We glanced over. She wasn't there. Half a mile farther up, the stream turned behind a boulder. The captain called out to the girl. There was no answer. We couldn't hear the sound of crying, either. We dashed off and reached the boulder together. The girl wasn't there, either. The stream, with no bushes around it, flowed straight to the middle of the prairie. The captain yelled, "Neda! . . . Neda! . . ." and I saw the drops of blood. A cluster of drops, farther up another drop, and then farther away again another drop. We looked up and on the mountain ridge we saw the pink of the girl's dress. Captain Meena yelled out again. I don't know if he had seen the leopard or not. I was dumbfounded, and the pink dress was climbing higher and higher. It was as if the wind were gently carrying it away. . . . No, no, don't rush. That unknown darkness that I mentioned is not here. You must be patient. Give your lips to this mimosa-wood opium pipe and lend your ears to me. . . .

Midnight came and we were still pursuing the leopard. By dawn we had lost the trail of the girl's blood, or perhaps she had run out of blood. After all, how much blood could there be in a child's body? In vain, we kept shouting out. By early evening, tens of men with lanterns had set out after us. We could see the glow of their lanterns. They were climbing up the mountain in a harvest line, and the captain frantically clambered higher and dragged me along with him. Every ten or twenty feet he would stop and, mad with rage, hurl rocks in all directions. It was as if he wanted to break the mountain, to prevent an incident that had hours ago ended with the strike of a leopard's paw. His shouts sounded like pleas. This is what disturbed me. Was he pleading to the mountain or to the leopard? And rocks and rocks, and more rocks . . .

We had no inkling of where we were going. Pebbles

kept skipping out from under our feet. Our knees and elbows were cut. The Seven Sisters had unsuspectingly, or indifferently, turned. The crescent moon went on its way and now and then the wind brought the wails of a woman from the foot of the mountain. Near dawn, the captain dropped to his knees. Perhaps he had finally believed what had happened. Perhaps he was hoping he would wake up. By the time the sun rose, it was me who was dragging him along. There are thornbushes with beautiful pink flowers that from a distance look like a pink dress, and just these are enough for one to wander around for an entire day. The men from the village caught up with us. They had brought my rifle. But the leopard had disappeared. At nightfall I took the captain down the mountain by force.

On the evening of the second night, I told him to be strong. The villagers had found his daughter's stripped and masticated bones. Dazed and despondent, he stared at them. We quickly wrapped them up in a piece of white canvas and turned our eyes away from the man who was at a loss for what to do. I admired him. No one saw a single tear in his eyes. If it had been otherwise, he wouldn't be my friend. . . . After opium, tea with sugar candy hits the spot. . . . The captain's relatives and his wife's family came to the village. During this entire time, the woman had wept and wailed and the captain had kept silent. When the time came for them to leave, as he was climbing into the car, I asked him when he would return. He stared at me. I said, "You have to come back." With a strange voice, he asked, "What for?" I replied, "To kill the leopard. It's your right." He remained silent. But his wife held out her hands like claws and slurred something that sounded like "Kill it . . . kill it, tear it to pieces. . . ." She was holding out her hands as if she wanted to pluck out the leopard's eyes. The captain looked in amazement at the woman's unsheathed claws. The woman scratched at his face and screamed, "Kill it, kill it! . . ." I said, "I'll wait a week for you to kill it if you want. If you don't return, I'll go after it myself and send you its head." The car drove off. We stood there for a long time staring at the dust that rose in its wake. It was as if in that haze that moved away we could hear the voice of a woman screaming over and over again, "Kill it, kill it! . . ."

From that day on, I started gathering information about the leopard. A month earlier, a shepherd had seen it near the village. For years I had known there was a leopard in the mountains around the waterfall—a mateless and reclusive leopard that left people alone. I learned that old age had drawn it to the outskirts of the village, a place where without the agility of youth it could hunt for meat. Other than this, all the rifles that after the revolution had ended up in the hands of anyone and everyone had made hunting prey extinct. An old and hungry leopard . . . I told the villagers not to go near the waterfall. A leopard that has savored the ease of hunting man becomes a man-eater. I ordered cartridges for the Remington 270 to be brought from town and I sat with my eye on the road, waiting for Captain Meena to return. On the seventh day, he came, his eyes bloodshot, his hands shaking, and his jaw locked. I showed him the Remington. We went outside the village and with two shots adjusted the scope. I told the captain, "You have to bring it down yourself. I will go with you just to watch." He said, "I want to go alone." I said, "You can't." He told me how in the snowy mountain ranges of the west, at night he would wrap himself in white canvas and go looking for Iraqi dugouts. Two commandos for each two-person dugout. Just like a leopard, they would quietly creep up behind the sleeping enemy and swing the metal wire, the garrote, around his neck, and with one swift tug the guard's head would roll onto his chest. I said, "That leopard is not a scrawny Iraqi soldier. Someone has to be your guide." He yelled, "No! I want neither your sympathy nor—" He said, "All by myself, I will torture it to death." He fell silent and gazed out at the mountain. I was a bit concerned. Arguing with a man who even under these circumstances remains dry-eyed requires caution. Before he went to sleep, he took out a piece of pink fabric from his breast pocket and smelled it. In the middle of the night, he started to wheeze and jolted awake. He didn't tell me what he had dreamed, but the sound that came from his throat reminded me of the raspings of a throat that has suddenly been slit by a steel wire and, unawares, still inhales and exhales. Early the next morning, before he left, I told him, "Aim either at the center of its forehead or at its heart, so that it drops dead instantly. If you only wound it, it won't stop until it slaughters you." I told him about the power of a leopard's claw, which can break a man's neck with a single blow, and of its long leap. He scoffed. I could see in his eyes that he was planning to shoot the leopard in its spine, just as we had done to that deer. It was a kind of revenge. One could then approach the leopard and butcher it eye-to-eye while it was still alive. But I wasn't sure he'd be a match for the leopard.

This smoke you exhale intoxicates me, too. You have strong lungs, in one go. . . . I enjoy the play of the lips when they blow out the smoke and change its direction several times. You city people don't have to worry about shortness of breath; you can overindulge. Please, go ahead. . . . For a huntsman, it's easy to imagine a lone hunter in the mountain. The mountain itself tells the hunter where to scope out, how to clear the path and advance. The hunter's sweat is pleasant. A delicious thirst awakens in his throat. Little by little he starts to talk to the oddly shaped boulders, to the bushes. How beautiful you are, goat's thorn. You, rain-washed earth, show me a new footprint or fresh dung. . . . But the leopard, too, lies in ambush. With that yellow fur, it's hard to tell it apart from rocks and the raw terrain, especially when one's eyes burn with hatred. The captain had taken three days' worth of rations. From the second day, I was waiting to hear the sound of gunfire from the mountain. The sound of a single shot would be a sign of victory, and long silence would be a warning that he had been blindsided, after which I would have to set out to find my friend and my rifle. I wouldn't have minded shooting the leopard myself and sending its skin to the captain's wife. Of course, only if my friend would not come to any harm.

The third day passed, too. Together with two old hunters, we had set up camp near the waterfall. We kept a fire going throughout the night—a fire very different from our fire tonight. On the third night, I sat alone all night. The dark and shadowy mountain had concealed much of the starry sky. It was mysterious. Somewhere up there was a leopard that had tasted human flesh, and someplace else there was a man who had lost the serenity of his soul. The two, like two secrets, were hidden from sight in the darkness of the rocks. The mountain crest, like the serrated blade of a knife, bordered the dark blue sky. The captain had told me that he constantly saw the expression on his daughter's face the moment when the leopard's jaws opened near her head, and I constantly imagined him fallen on the ground, unavenged, with his jugular drained of blood. Not long into the morning, we heard the sound of a single shot and then the roar of the leopard. We set out toward the point where the sounds had come from. Two hours later, we saw the captain. He was falling, stumbling, rising again, and leaving a trail of blood behind. We lifted him up onto our shoulders and carried him to the village. His left cheek had been slashed by the leopard's claw. On the same side, his clothes were torn and his shoulder was lacerated. We rubbed ointment on his wounds and bandaged them. Not many people who slip up manage to escape a leopard. Well, when you see the leopard going to its den after its nightly hunt, and it's within range of your rifle, just aim the plus sign of the scope right under its ear or on its paw and shoot. Why would you go any closer, especially when you have your back to the wind? If you move closer, you will at once realize that no matter how much you scope around among the rocks and bushes, you can no longer detect that shade of yellow that brings to mind the color of fire at midday, and then you suddenly hear a sound that resembles a mucus-filled cough and you see a yellow flash lunging at you. . . .

I showed the captain the leopard's bite mark on the stock of my beloved rifle so that he would see how it had pierced through walnut wood. "It would have dug down to your bone if it had gotten hold of your neck." He looked at me and said nothing. That night, he slept as peacefully as a child. Perhaps his nightmares had spilled out of him along with his blood, or perhaps having fought again had calmed him down. Once in a while we would hear the roar of the leopard coming from far away. It was probably calling to its mate from when it was young, or to something more powerful than itself—if leopards believe in a mightier power up above. After taking a delayed shot at the leopard that had lunged at him, the captain had turned the rifle around to strike at its jaw. His warrior instinct had taken over, and by the time the beast released its teeth from the rifle stock, the captain had drawn his army combat knife. He said he attacked the leopard with his knife. I didn't believe him. Perhaps the leopard was accidentally wounded after its second assault. . . . The scars on the captain's cheek and shoulder suggested that the leopard had thrown him to the ground. No matter how many times I asked him what had happened after that moment, he wouldn't tell me. He never explained how they had both managed to escape alive. Three days later, I took the rifle to go put the leopard out of its misery. He understood. He said, "I will kill whoever goes near that leopard." And he dragged himself out of bed. I told him, "You're laid up; don't do anything stupid." He said, "Cuts from a leopard's claws are no worse than wounds from mortar shrapnel." He stood up. He was cursing at heaven and earth. He even wanted to get into a fight with me.

I like everything in the world to be clear and obvious to me. Revenge is an obvious issue. It is one's right. I wiped the leopard's blood from the captain's combat knife and handed it to him so that he would calm down. He had kicked out the old woman who was tending to his wounds. He had even beaten up a servant. I said, "Everything is clear; I agree that the leopard's blood is yours by right." Finally, he went to sleep. During those three days, fearing the wounded leopard, no shepherd had taken his herd out to graze. Most of the farmers had stayed home, too. In the middle of the fourth night, we woke up to the shouts of the villagers. Armed with clubs and lanterns, they were standing in groups along the dirt road. Their terrified looks angered Captain Meena and me. The sheep, having smelled a leopard, were huddled together and rasping in the folds. And at the far end of the dirt road, a dog lay on the ground with its jugular slashed. The captain, dragging his leg, walked out of the village. He stood before the dark mountain. A razor-shaped crescent moon stood above the mountain crest and the sky around it was empty of stars. I said, "I can't keep these villagers quiet any longer than this. They want to go after the leopard." He scoffed, "All this for one leopard?" I had no answer to offer. Then, after he had stood there staring at the specter of the mountain for some time, he explained that during his fray with the leopard, for a few seconds they had locked eyes. He spoke of the leopard's amber eyes, of their coldness, of the icy flames that lived in those eyes. To me, it was incomprehensible. . . . I have never locked eyes with a leopard. I would never even allow one to come close to me. The captain said he saw that look when he stabbed it with his knife. As he spoke, I kept looking around, for fear that a pair of blazing eyes might be staring at us from somewhere in the dark. Gently, I told him that in the dark, standing beside his old friend, a man may shed a few tears. One can cry for a child because children are weak and innocent creatures. As if he had suddenly remembered, he yelled out at the mountain, "Neda! . . . Neda! . . ." In the midst of his cries, his voice broke and no answer came from the mountain. . . .

Three days later, we set out together. I had underestimated his physical strength. He was weak, but he kept going and dragged me along with him. He had made it a condition that I not bring a rifle. His bereavement and the expression on his face, which with the scars from the leopard's paw gave him an air of insanity, had made me obedient. There was one other reason. I wanted him to have this opportunity, so that if he were to fail, he would come to fully accept it. I was carrying a heavy backpack, to which the villagers had tied a baby goat. Shortly after noon, we reached the place where the captain and the leopard had fought. We tethered the young animal to a rock beside a shallow streamlet and climbed up to a point where we would have a clear field of vision. We would take turns with the binoculars, looking in every direction, especially in the direction of the bait. At some point, while watching the rambunctious baby goat, the captain said, "It's just like the booby traps the Iraqis used to plant for us. One rifle, one combat knife . . . whoever picked it up would go flying into the air. Except that this trap's explosives are right here in my rifle." And he slapped the rifle with his hand. He sounded gruff and his expression puzzled me. It was as if he was and was not there. An unsuspecting lizard slithered up to our feet and scurried into a goat's thorn. We saw no sign of the leopard until nightfall. We could see the flickering glow of the fires the villagers had lit around the village, and the captain was saying that the child had meant something special to him. He was saying that as a sharpshooter, he always used to volunteer for missions, but after the birth of his daughter, he had grown more cautious and would only occasionally climb the heights facing the Iraqis. He would wait in ambush, take one of them out, and return. We started debating whether it is better to kill someone when the person is unaware or in face-to-face combat. He insisted that a soldier at war is never unaware and that he should at all times, even when he leaves the trench to relieve himself, expect a sniper's bullet to wipe him out. I asked, "How many?" He said, "Seven. Three of them were probably officers." I asked, "Then why didn't you shoot the leopard when you saw it from a distance?" Grudgingly, he raised the binoculars to his eyes. The baby goat was not quieting down. In the dark, it was a sign that its head had not yet been crushed. . . . No, a man should never question his friend's wishes. From long ago, it had been our pact never to disregard each other's wishes. Whoever made a wish first.

The moon rose in the sky and we could vaguely see down the mountain. It was a cool night. I told the captain, "If you don't tear up the leopard's skin, it will make a nice blanket for your next child." He said, "I'll crush its bones the same way it . . ." He suddenly grew silent. I didn't realize what was going through his mind. We decided to take shifts. I couldn't sleep; I regretted that I didn't have a rifle at my side. At times like this, a rifle gives one peace of mind. . . . Have you ever considered why on nights such as this we come to notice the sky? What if it's because the sky has no simple answers to offer us? . . . In the middle of the night, the captain asked, "What else do you think there could be in the eyes of a leopard other than cruelty?" I said, "Perhaps the colorlessness of death." He said, "No, there's something else in them that troubles me."

Near dawn, I fell asleep. In sleep, it seemed as if I could hear a leopard breathing. Breaths heavy with the mass and the power concentrated in its chest. It seemed to be close to me. So close that a few times I thought I smelled its breath. It was a mix of spoiled meat, fur, and rain-washed earth. . . . I jolted awake at the sound of a breechblock. It was morning; the captain was taking aim. I quickly looked through the binoculars. The leopard was standing near the bait. I whispered, "Let's wait until it takes the meat and starts walking away; we will approach it diagonally." With one strike, the leopard silenced the goat and started eating it right there. It was obviously very hungry. We moved down to a point where we were sure one bullet would do the job. The captain again took aim. I was keeping an eye on the leopard through the binoculars. How I wished I were the one holding the rifle, so that I could taste the tension before pulling the trigger. I whispered, "Under its ear . . ." From the edge of the binoculars' eyepiece I glanced at the captain and the aimed rifle, and then at the leopard. With a swing of its neck, it tore off a piece of flesh and devoured it. Once in a while it would raise its head and smell the air. Motionless. To every hunter's liking. The captain had half-cocked the hammer. I said, "Shoot, go ahead and shoot!" The leopard, as if it had heard, turned and looked in our direction. Now one could aim at that perfect space between its eyes. With great effort, I kept my voice low. "Shoot, damn it!" The captain aimed, and holding his aim, he stalled. It was as if he had turned to stone. I reached out to take the rifle from him. Without turning his face or changing his expression, he growled like a leopard. Again, I looked through the binoculars. The goat's liver was dangling from the corner of its jaw and its eyes were glued in our direction. The early sun glowed in those eyes. They had turned the color of pure agate. I begged, "Shoot it! It's waiting for you to shoot it. . . . It knows. . . . Shoot!" And I pressed the binoculars to my eyes to witness the instant when the bullet impacted the leopard's fore-head. To witness how its head shattered, how it was thrown back, and how its legs trembled in the air for a while and then finished . . . But the sound of a bullet being fired never came.

At that moment, I understood the strange and weighty silence of the mountain. I looked over at the captain. He had knotted his eyebrows. His cheek was pressed against the rifle stock. His neck was slightly bent, as if he had rested his head on a lover's shoulder, and he was pressing the butt of the rifle tight against his shoulder. The sun was shining from behind the hand that held the trigger. The thick black hair on his hand shimmered. The veins on the back of his hand had enlarged, and I stared to see when there would be movement in them and the trigger would be pulled. I said, "Shoot, you flop, your kid . . . shoot . . . shat-ter its teeth. . . . ." I yelled, "Your kid, damn you . . . Shoot for her!" And then I scrambled to look through the binoculars again. The leopard was still standing there. One paw on the goat's cadaver, its head raised, it was looking in our direction. Its flaming color had been painted with black dots, each of which could have been a bullet hole. The leopard yawned; its teeth glistened. The sound of a shot rang out. But the leopard did not budge. I thought either the bullet had missed or the leopard was so strong that . . . After the second shot, the leopard was unscathed. It was staring straight at us. After the third shot, too. I threw the binoculars on the ground and only then saw that the captain was holding the nozzle up in the air and was discharging the bullets one after the other. All of them. And then he put the rifle down. I don't know how much time passed between us. I came to when it dawned on me that we were sitting there with no bullets, close to a leopard. I looked up. Peaceful and proud, and perhaps slightly limping, it was climbing up. Its bulk behind a boulder or a bush would turn into rock or bush, and still farther away it would turn into flames, into amber. The captain, worn-out, had started moving in the opposite direction, moving down. It was the mountain that was pulling him. I slung the rifle over my shoulder and followed him. He was tired, his knees were giving way, and he was stumbling. Yet he didn't have the appearance of a defeated soldier in retreat. That unknown darkness that I mentioned is right here. *Darkness* may not be an appropriate word. I don't know. I call things that are not clear and obvious to me "darkness." I don't like them. The world's goings-on must be evident. Everyone should know what the answer to everything is. Inhales and exhales, thirst and satiation, friendship and friendship, enmity and enmity . . .

We still have some burning charcoal. . . . Could someone please open a window to let in the early-morning air. . . . I don't know. That leopard is still up in the mountain and I don't know what I'm supposed to do. My rifle is geared up; the exhaustion of those days has left me. I'm fit and ready for a hunt. But I don't know. . . . I saw the captain climbing down the mountain. I caught up with him. I wanted to take his arm. Angrily, he smacked my hand away. I grabbed onto his shoulders and shouted, "Why didn't you shoot?" I wanted to throw a punch at him. He didn't answer. I again shouted, "You flop, why didn't you kill it? You wasted your child's blood." His knees buckled. He leaned against a boulder. He groaned, "It was impossible." I didn't let go of him. I dug my fingers deeper into his shoulders. "Damn you, why didn't you shoot?" He yelled, "I couldn't . . . I just couldn't. My child's flesh is in its body. . . . My child's blood runs in its veins. . . . I couldn't." And he cried silently all the way down the mountain.

Seven Captains

I HAD WRITTEN, "DON'T COME BACK! If you do, they'll nail you. They'll kill you like a dog." I had written, "You miserable swine, at least you're alive overseas. Have your fun; don't come back. . . ." I had written, "I don't want to get caught up in this mess." And I had written, "Twenty-two years is nothing; even a hundred years won't be enough to wash away the bad blood and simmer down the tribe's fury. . . . Don't come back!"

In the small arrivals hall of the airport, I can't find him among the passengers of the beat-up Fokker. When everyone charges toward the pile of suitcases, I see him. He is standing next to the entrance like a statue. His beautiful hair has turned thin and gray, but like old times, he keeps it long. He has aged much more than I'd imagined . . . much older . . . with dark glasses that hide his eyes. I can't tell if he is afraid, nervous, or just guilt-ridden. I say, "Your suitcase . . . go get it and let's get out of here."

He doesn't make a move. I'm short of breath. He says, "It's a small blue suitcase."

"I'm not your kid lackey anymore. Go get your suitcase before someone sees us."

He doesn't move. My eyes burn from last night's sleeplessness. I stare at his glasses and finally I understand. Behind that darkness there is something dead and decayed.

He slaps away my hand. Dragging his feet, in the stir of the air behind me, he walks out of the airport. Even now that autumn has come, this bastard sun still manages to rot everything from behind the clouds. Without my help, he gets into the car. I wonder if he's playing me for a fool. In third gear, I say, "I kept writing, 'Don't come back. . . . There's nothing left for you here.'"

"I have to go to Seven Captains. . . . Take me to Seven Captains."

"What? You want to go treasure hunting? With eyes that hardly see? . . . I don't care who takes you, but it won't be me."

He reaches out, searching for my hand.

"What was *gillyflower* code for?"

I just blurted it out.

"You have nothing to worry about. You're the tribe's favorite. You serve them all. . . . I've heard they respect you a lot. Why are you so spineless? Don't be a bastard. Drive me to Seven Captains."

"You, for one, shouldn't be calling me a bastard. You're my guest; I fear for your life."

"My life? . . . The hell with it!"

After years of being free from it all, again for the thousandth time, Kokab, huddled in the corner of the room, lifts her head up from her knees. Fist marks . . . dark black blotches on a face as beautiful as the full moon; her eyes, darker still. Again, those ominous eyes stare at me. . . . Again, I shove a bowl of food in front of her. Around her, old dishes have grown moldy. Whatever those eyes have to say, it's beyond the heart and mind of a young boy.

Of course I couldn't understand. I was only eleven. Of course I couldn't understand what her stubborn eyes were asking.

"Tell me what the town looks like. Are there still separate knockers for men and women on the front doors? Are there still revolutionary slogans on the walls?"

"We're around your old neighborhood. Since the nuclear power plant got going again, most of the buildup has shifted over there. These old neighborhoods . . . just imagine, one by one the houses have been abandoned and one by one they're falling into ruin."

"Who's died in recent years? The battalion of uncles . . . does the tribe's baby-hatching machine still mass-produce?"

"I told your brothers you're coming. They said they'd come only to greet your corpse."

The sun and the rain have bleached the old revolutionary slogans on the walls lining the street I'm driving along. Some have been crossed out, replaced by new ones.

"Year after year, during all these years that have passed, my eyes slowly burned. In the West, where you said I should just have fun, if there was any happiness for anyone, there was none for me. My eyes gradually burned and turned into ashes. But even through these ashes I still see Kokab. Why didn't she run away at night? . . . In the middle of that crowd, why did she come out? . . . You bastard! Take me to Seven Captains."

He sounds weary. He sounds like he has been crying.

"Seven Captains isn't that smugglers' lair anymore. Scrap whatever you remember, scrap it all. It's changed a lot. They leveled all those mud huts and built engineer-designed houses. One of these days they're going to pave the town square and all the roads around it, too. Now, right in the middle of the square, right where Kokab fell, they're laying out flower beds, planting violets. In the winter, the flowers will grow as big as the palm of your hand."

"Do you remember what *violet* was code for?"

"I was just the messenger; it's not like I was in on your secrets."

"*Violet* meant the fish market, from early morning until whenever she could come. Even if she came at noon, I'd still be there waiting. She came, pretending she had to buy fish. She would weave her way through the fishmongers' stands and I would follow her. Even now, whenever I want to see it, in the darkness of my eyes, I still can. When her beautiful pale hand came out from under her chador, among the glitter of fish scales and ice . . . To me her hands were made of the same substance as the moon. I would run my fingers over every fish she had touched. Sometimes I would plot my course so that I would end up facing her, so that our eyes would meet for one instant . . . and sometimes, no matter how long I waited, she wouldn't come. The fish

would all be sold, the large trays would empty, the ice
would melt . . . the fishmongers would leave."

Kokab's eyes . . . staring, questioning, boring into
me . . . I turn the wheel as hard as I can. I didn't see
the old man in the middle of the road. I almost got
stuck having to pay his blood money. This cursed
scum plunked down next to me . . . his entire being is
repulsive. To piss him off, I say, "Now we're in front
of Gheisarieh Jewelers. Your bad luck was contagious;
the poor guy caught it, too. He hit tough times. One of
those sharks who got rich after the revolution bought
him out for next to nothing."

"That pearl . . . it was a bad omen. But when I
saw it in the shop window, it seemed to have magic. I
couldn't pass it up. It was stupid of me to hand it
over to you. . . . Otherwise, Kokab could have been in
Hamburg right now, waiting for me. I could have been
here visiting my family and I would hurry back to her.
Maybe nothing would have happened."

I can't believe he is actually capable of getting
choked up. My hands are sweaty. They slip on the
steering wheel. I'm afraid he'll hear the trembling of
my body in my voice.

"We're now near Irvan Liquor Store. For a few
years after you ran off, your friend Sergei used to
secretly ask about you. When I would tell him that
I had no news, he'd say you turned out to be a bastard, too. Your only ally was the town's Armenian
booze peddler. Now his store has turned into Sadaf
Ice Cream Shop. . . . You want some?"

"If Sergei is there."

"You're dreaming! . . . Even after the revolution, the guy wouldn't give up. They arrested him twice for making booze."

"Sergei really understood. He used to say if a man is a real man, he can tell the difference between love and shoving a boner in a cesspit."

I wipe my hands on my pants. Again Kokab's eyes, in a slashed face, search for me, so that again she can stare into my eyes and struggle to read my mind.

"When Kokab sent a message saying *petunia*, what was it code for?"

"It meant that the next evening at dusk, we'd meet at Captain Heshmat's house. He had petunias in his garden. I made a point of going there two or three times a week to smoke a water pipe and to listen to the old man go on and on, so that he wouldn't wonder why I always happened to be there when Kokab came to bring medicine for his wife. All I looked forward to was for Kokab to come and sit next to us, pretending to ask about the captain's health. The old man's eyes couldn't see very well. Kokab and I talked without uttering a word. We could read each other's lips. . . . We'd talk to each other, and for the hundredth time, Captain Heshmat would tell us about the great feats of his Brno rifle in the battle with Britain's Indian mercenaries. . . . Toward the end, Kokab and I could sometimes read each other's eyes."

The scoundrel, he never told me about his carrying on with Kokab. He probably thought some poor beggar boy didn't deserve to know such things . . . but I

would have understood. Two dilapidated colonial buildings stand like a gateway on either side of the narrow
Khayyam Street; the sea suddenly appears between
them. He turns his face to the window, and as if he has
smelled the salty water, he groans: "The sea?"

"From the coastal road they've built a boulevard all
the way to the other end of town. If you had any sight
left in your eyes, you'd see what a great job they've done.
It's where people hang out these days, the tourists. . . ."

"The town smells different. I'm sure it's cloudy
now . . . isn't it? I smell rain in the air. But I can tell,
the sea smells different, too."

The gray of the clouds reflects on the strangely
quiet sea. I see without seeing: dead fish, silver-colored,
floating belly-up . . . tiny black fish nibbling at them . . .
the glitter of Kokab's dress next to her gillyflowers. I'm
itching to ask, Aunt Kokab, can we have a code, too?

"There were very few lights here; it was always dark
at night. On nights when the sea was stormy, when the
waves beat against the seawall, seawater would splash
onto the roadway. I was here. The water thrashing
against me. It was soothing."

"Maybe you thought you were being washed of
your filth."

"I really liked this stretch of the road. In the dark,
it felt like a foreign port, like someplace far away, mysterious. I spent many nights walking here, imagining
Kokab strolling next to me. . . . I would even imagine
the wind whipping her hair against my face."

I don't want to remember . . . no, I really don't

want to remember. I don't want to see her drenched in
ill-fated sweat. . . . I don't want to remember, so that
I won't come to the seashore again in the middle of
the night . . . all those nights, standing there, drained
and worn-out. Now I know that the darkness of the sea
at night is not empty. Unknown things wander around
in it—ghosts of the drowned, fears, secrets, hopes that
lovers have entrusted to the waves, divine punishments
waiting to descend from heaven. The darkness of Kokab's eyes, like the darkness of the sea at night, spreads
all around me. I see her face, as beautiful as the full
moon. . . . I see her eye burst. The seagulls stubbornly
peck at a carcass in the middle of the road. As the car
approaches, they fly away. In the rearview mirror, I see
them return and sit in the middle of the road again.

"When you were at the nuclear power plant, there
was talk that you had something secret going on with a
German lady engineer. I knew what something secret
meant. But I couldn't figure out why, when you had a
foreign lady engineer, then why Kokab, too? . . ."

In my head, again the dull thud of stone hitting
flesh . . . again, I return to the barbed wire fence around
the nuclear power plant. The soldier on guard aims
his rifle at me and curses at me to stay away. Behind
him the giant plant, its scaffolding and the bare steel
of its incomplete dome under the sun . . . it's as if the
hands of a giant have woven it all together. It's very
strange, ominous in a way that I cannot understand. It
frightens me. . . . The soldiers guarding it don't let local
brats wander around there. Every time I come with a

message from Kokab, they drive me away, and still I
go back. The sun-beaten asphalt softly gives way under
my feet. I worry that the hot tar will seep through the
seams of my shoes and my feet will be covered with
yellow blisters again. He finally walks out of the gates,
wearing his strange outfit. The wind in his long hair,
his figure the same as the German engineers'. When he
strokes my head, I want something to happen so that I
can fight for him, so that I can give my life for him. He
says, "Tell Kokab, definitely . . ."

"That German woman just wanted to have some
fun while she was in Iran. . . . About the day Kokab
died . . . do you remember anything? Anything important you haven't told me?"

I curse and turn the wheel so hard that he jerks
sideways and hits his head against the window.

"It's nothing. A seagull jumped in the middle of
the road."

I pull over. The coastal road is empty. There's little
chance that any of the relatives will see us here, but I
still look around carefully. He gets out of the car and
walks toward the water. A wet wind is blowing from
the sea. It cools my burning face and whips at his frail
figure. The waves, glazed with a rainbow of grease,
smash against the seawall and splash on our faces.

"Somewhere around here there are stone stairs that
lead down to the water. . . . Take me there."

When the tide is low, the last steps of the staircase
emerge from the sea. Tiny snails have turned into stone
on them.

"Kokab was supposed to make her way here. For seventeen nights, I waited for her, in the dark. If she had run away and come to me, they would never have gotten their hands on her."

I have to tell him that I have no scores to settle and hold no grudges against anyone. When I say hello, I want to get a response. Even if I don't, I still say good-bye as I leave. I have to tell him that construction at the power plant has brought jobs and money to town and that a trickle of it comes my way. With a small contracting business, I make enough to feed my guests well, and I can save what little is left so that when the time comes, I can leave this town forever . . . as if I had never been here. I will tell him I don't remember much about twenty-two years ago. I'll say, "What do you expect? Being as scrawny as I was, in the middle of that crowd around the square at Seven Captains, I kept being pushed and shoved, I kept falling. Everyone was clamoring to see blood." I'll tell him, "You miserable swine, after all these years, how am I supposed to know whether I actually saw everything I remember or whether it all got into my head from the stories people told?"

But I tell him that I saw it all. From among the crowd that surrounded Kokab, I saw it all so clearly. I still see it. Suddenly, unexpectedly, like a miracle . . . or maybe as a sign of divine wrath . . . a whirlwind, maybe Satan's storm, rips Kokab's chador off her head, twists it up, and pulls it away. Kokab still hasn't fallen to her knees, but the whirlwind flies her black chador above the crowd, toward the sea. And before the sand

and salt whipping through the air burn our eyes, we all see that evil wonder . . . golden, wave upon wave. We all see that dreadful mane. Abundant, glistening . . . from every strand of Kokab's hair, thin lines of blood streaming down onto her pale neck and chest.

Now that he has come back to the car, I should just drive away from this place. I should take him for a ride outside of town until it gets dark. Then I can dump him at the bus terminal for Tehran and get on with my life.

"There are night buses to Tehran. You have to leave before word gets out that you're here. Even now, if they get their hands on you, they'll spill your blood."

"After we go to Seven Captains . . . after Seven Captains . . ."

"You really wouldn't mind if they nailed you, would you? Is this what you came back for? If it is, I don't want to have anything to do with it this time."

"What do you remember from that day?"

"Enough to know that taking messages back and forth for you and Kokab was sort of like pimping."

"Shut up!"

The blind man throws a punch. . . . His mouth is full of growls. . . . Four bloodstains on the windshield . . . By the time I open the car door, he's still punching the windshield. I grab him by the collar to drag him out. The pathetic sap clutches onto the seat with both hands. I yank harder. His glasses fall on the car floor. . . . His eyes . . . they look like they're filled with ashes. . . . I slam the door shut. . . . Glittering scales of mangled fish float on the sea. The wind is still whipping drops of seawater against my face. Maybe it's because of them that I manage to swallow my rage like phlegm after a cough. Just like all those years of my life that have passed by and gone away. All those years in the lonely solitude of celibacy, dreaming of a life and a home like everyone else, dreaming of getting married.

Streams of water, bathed in light, rain down on the gillyflowers like silvery sparkles. When she sees me, Kokab puts the heavy watering can down on the edge of her flower bed. There's little time left before nightfall, when the gillyflowers will open and fill the yard with their perfume. Kokab quickly glances at the house. The windows . . . She has told me to watch out for the ulcerated eyes of the old women Captain Jalal sends to help her out around the house. . . . They're everywhere; they see everything. When I see Kokab next to the flower bed that she loves as much as the child she never had, I tell myself that instead of whispering *violet*, I should ask, "Aunt Kokab, aren't you going to plant any violets in your garden?" . . . Kokab's approving smile fills me with pride. . . . Kokab, head-to-toe beads of light. The setting sun happily, merrily, reflects off the sequins on her local dress. I sense her joy at having received the message. My small body fills with manliness from the touch of her finger against my cheek. And behind the window, like two dark cavities, I see the blacks of an old woman's eyes watching us. "Come, let's go inside. It's been ten days since I put some ice cream in the fridge for you." Her voice, calm and soft, always bears the sorrow of loneliness, isolation. Behind us, the tin watering can falls off the edge of the flower bed. Water spills onto the hot bricks and flows along the grooves between them. I hear it sizzle.

I don't remember when I started the car, and I really don't know where the hell to take him. Suddenly, he reaches for the steering wheel. I grip it tight.

"Why did you turn? If you just go straight, we'll arrive at Seven Captains."

"They've made this stretch of the road one-way. I have to turn onto the lower road."

"To go to Seven Captains?"

As though I want him to see, I nod. He lets go of the steering wheel.

Once in a while, a few dusty raindrops fall on the windshield. It's better not to turn on the wipers and to just watch them glide sideways to the edge of the glass. Sometimes, before they reach the edge, they dry up and leave a streak of grime behind. Kokab, squatting down under the window . . . When I open the door, her eyes stare directly into mine. It's as if she has been waiting for me. In the hallway, the old women come and go. One of them had said, "Give the grub and water to this little brat to take to her instead of the pearl." . . . And Kokab's eyes are staring at me. I turn around and look behind. An old woman with cataract eyes is warily watching me. . . . I suddenly realize I have driven to the outskirts of town.

"We're leaving town now. The sea is still to our right. Far away, a cargo ship, one of those ocean liners, has dropped anchor. Maybe it's broken down. . . . The beach here . . . to tell you the truth, Seven Captains looks nothing like it used to."

"Is the town square still there?"

"The sea there is filled with garbage and slime. It stinks so bad, no one can stand it."

Maybe he doesn't feel pain. His knuckles . . . from the punches, his knuckles are caked with blood. Flanking the coastal road, the mud huts start. From inside the darkness of their windows, eyes stare out. Even trachomatous eyes can see who's in the car.

His voice sounds more like a groan. "It's not right for you to talk about Kokab like this. . . . Don't say these things about our relationship. One night when she knew I was wandering around the seawall, she took a huge risk and came there, so that she could make my dream of walking alongside her come true. She walked with me, but her face was wet with tears."

"Kokab grew dearer to you day by day. You only remembered me when you wanted to send messages back and forth."

"Kokab was too good for this town. If they hadn't married her off to that captain so soon, I would have found her, married her. She was too good for that peasant smuggler."

"Whatever she was or wasn't, she belonged to her husband."

"They couldn't stand the sight of her. They turned against her just because she was different from everyone else."

We drive through Del Pir's sparse palm grove.

Here and there, a few of the trees have tilted down toward the earth. They look like they're about to come up by their roots. The wind has piled mounds of sand around the mud huts.

"Do you remember Del Pir? . . . Its people are still here. . . . The government was no match for them, not with money, not by force. The government has bought all the land around the nuclear power plant, but the locals here won't budge from their mud huts."

"They suddenly pour out of their huts, moldy people, more than a thousand of them, screaming things I don't understand. They surround me. There's always some strange rage in their eyes. They stare at me and then, as though obeying an order they alone can hear, they reach down for rocks. . . . You didn't think the blind can dream, did you? . . . Blind people like me dream of these people and their mud huts, too."

Driving along the endless road, I don't know where to go. On the power plant's air-defense fortification, a soldier slumped over an antiaircraft machine gun is smoking a cigarette. He stares at us.

"Now we're in front of the power plant. Ever since the Russian engineers came, they want to finish its construction and get it over with. There's talk that the Westerners have said they'll bomb it. If they do, people say we'll all die. . . . Do you think they're right?"

He smirks. I don't know if he's laughing at us dying or what. The tall dome of the power plant has risen in the sky. . . sturdy and strong.

"You drunkard, the adulterer that you were, you

forgot all about God and Prophet. You weren't short of women. Living the fast life, engineer at the nuclear power plant, rubbing shoulders with Westerners, lots of prestige and a huge salary. What were you missing in life that you had to go after Kokab?"

"That same thing that the more money and status you have, the more you miss."

"Captain Jalal was like a father to me."

I shout in his face: "You bastard, you know you're lying when you say he was a peasant and a smuggler. He was a man this town respected. A lot of girls dreamed of becoming his wife. He stopped a lot of poor families from selling their girls to Arab sheikhs."

My hand closes into a fist in front of his face. The blind louse can't see well enough to be scared.

"He was proud and decent. . . . When you put the stamp of cuckold on his forehead, he was so shamed and dishonored that he went away and no one ever saw him again. Being blind isn't enough punishment for you. . . . It's not enough that you're stuck drifting around the world."

My hand, small and dirty, clenched into a fist . . . my fist opens to reveal the luster of a pearl before the disbelieving eyes of the captain. . . . I see myself opening my fist.

"You knew that with your handsome mug and damn Western ways, that poor woman would fall in love with you. Many of the decent women in town couldn't even dream of the grand life the captain had made for his Kokab. The poor man thought that once he had wrapped his Kokab in silk and gold, she wouldn't jump into someone else's filthy bed."

I slam on the brakes. In the middle of nowhere . . . this is what he deserves . . . right here. Right here where trucks dump the town's garbage and burn it.

"This is Seven Captains. . . . Right here is where Dey Hashem's house used to be. . . . I don't care if you get out of the car or not."

He walks away from the car. He stops. It's as though he doesn't have the stomach to go any farther. In the distance, the mounds of burned garbage are still smoldering.

He raises his hand and points toward them.

"From there! . . . So Kokab . . . Kokab was coming from there? . . . Why? . . . Why didn't she run away and come to me?"

The raindrops get bigger and turn into a downpour. They pound on the roof of the car, but it feels like they're pounding on my head, my head with no hair and no skin. What if my voice has made him suspicious . . . like a dog that sniffs around? . . . Go ahead, sniff, smell the garbage dump around you. . . . Payback for the blood of that poor naïve Kokab, whom you screwed. My punishment is Captain Jalal's heavy hand that pounds me in the mouth . . . my mouth on fire, my mouth full of blood and broken teeth. The captain's voice, monstrous, close to my ear: "So! Who's the bastard who sent the pearl? . . . You'd better tell me!" And then, just like a piece of crumpled cardboard, he drops to his knees, to the stump of his knees, that mass of masculinity and strength brought down to his knees for having been made a cuckold.

And it seems it's right now that he has burst into wailing sobs over the shame his wife has brought him. I jump up and run, run fast . . . run and fall, again and again, foolishly, fall and rise again and again, and I don't know whom to ask, "What should I do?" . . . I suddenly realize that I've unconsciously come running to this bastard. I'm telling him that the captain took the pearl out of my pocket . . . and despite my greenness, I know he has to run away; they'll kill him if he doesn't. I see, pale and desperate, he keeps asking me, a kid, what he should do. He grabs my hand. "Go, for the love of God, go to the captain's house. . . . Don't be afraid. They won't do anything to you. . . . If you love me, go to Kokab. They're probably beating her. . . . God, what happened? . . . Tell her, go to her and tell her *gillyflower* . . . just that. . . . She'll know what to do. . . . Don't forget, *gillyflower*." I can't believe it. The mightiest man, the wisest and most handsome man, is shaking like a scared and helpless dog.

Blind and ignorant, he thinks he's walking in the direction Kokab had come from. The rain beats against him. He turns back, frustrated. He wanders toward the sea, and again turns back. His hair is stuck to his face and his wet clothes are clinging to his body. He looks even frailer than before. He bends down, runs his hand over the earth. I want to laugh out loud, to laugh loud enough for him to hear my contempt.

He gets back into the car. His unseeing eyes are

on me. I reach over and with a tissue wipe the fog and blood off the windshield.

"Why did you bring me here? This isn't Seven Captains. . . ."

I get out of the car and walk toward the sea. I hear him behind me, trudging over the garbage on the beach . . . cans and plastic bottles, fruit peels, the innards of animals, used syringes, a doll's head. . . . He catches up with me and collapses on the sand.

For a minute, I think, If I kill him right here and burn his corpse, no one will ever know. . . .

"What is there left of me to make it worth your mockery?"

Someone grabs my hand in the dark. . . . My heart sinks in fear. I hear rasping breaths. Captain Jalal's gas lighter flicks on, its flame licks at the tip of a cigarette. I see his eyes, bloodred. . . . Glistening wet drops streaming down his face and in between strands of his beard. "Boy, you've really earned your bread." My thin wrist is still in his grip. Every minute seems like a year, time drags . . . until I think the pain in my wrist has faded away. I free my arm and quietly walk away. I still don't know whether the captain was being sarcastic or really meant what he said.

Waves of sludge and garbage come up to our feet.

"I was like the son the captain never had. I, too, was to blame for the shame his wife brought him. No matter who says, 'You were only a kid; you didn't know any better,' I know I was to blame. My shame is still in my blood, in my soul."

My fingers are like ten blades in the sand; I pull them out. He won't let me take his arm to help him across the piles of garbage. Dragging his feet, he follows me. In my mind, before my eyes, it has all started again. . . . I see hands and arms, faces of screaming people . . . and I hear the hiss of stones flying in the air. How do I know I didn't reach down and pick up a rock in Seven Captains square? It seems I'm shouting as loud as Captain Jalal's brother. "The damn whore won't die!" Six feet away from her, he raises a cinder block above his head and hurls it at her. "Die, you whore!" And I see that now, now I'm driving slowly. In front of us, on the horizon, the clouds are all torn up and behind them the sun is sinking into the sea. . . . A streak of blood streams down Kokab's forehead along her locks of hair. It streams down her forehead. . . .

"The days of waiting in Istanbul were bitter and dark. Every month they said, 'Your request for asylum will be approved next month.' I had a good reason for seeking asylum. Do you get it? Thanks to Kokab's death and the fact that an entire tribe was after me, I had a really good reason . . . and they could benefit from my knowledge of the nuclear power plant. . . . I thought I would forget. I thought I would start a new life. Little did I know my hell was only just beginning. Hamburg's port . . . I was constantly drawn to it, to sit and stare out at the water . . . water that in the end would unite with this sea."

The sun ripples as it dips into this sea.

"I told her, 'No matter what happens, don't ever

confess.' . . . I told her to deny any relationship with me so that no judge could sentence her. I told her it wasn't for my own sake. I wasn't married and my punishment would only be a lashing. But she . . . she knew. . . . Why did she confess? Why didn't she run away and come to me? All these years, all these questions . . ."

Kokab's eyes . . . I don't want to take food to her anymore, because she shamelessly gapes and stares into my eyes. Around her head, like a halo, her golden hair . . . No one has hair like hers, like a sign of blasphemy and ingratitude to God . . . not just punishment for her sin but punishment for even greater sins. The captains in the family, the elders of the tribe, their faces somber, deep in thought, out in the yard, in the rooms at Captain Jalal's house, sitting, smoking, waiting. Waiting for Captain Jalal to speak. The women, old and young, dressed in black. They know that their whispers reach the men, or are instilled in them: "They must behead her." . . . "No, her blood must not run on the earth." . . . "No, for adultery, religion demands that she be stoned. We must stone her." And the young men of the family, sailors obedient to the captain, their knives in their pockets, lying in ambush at street corners, searching from house to house for the man who dared screw the wife of a captain.

He is still ranting. "It was my choice. I thought . . . I mean . . . anyone who has the will can make their eyes turn into dry wells—"

I interrupt him. "We're there."

But I don't tell him that every time I come here, I park my car exactly where Kokab was staring that day.

In the distance, on the edge of the sea, even in this early-evening light, the large dome of the power plant shines white. Like a chariot from the sky . . . its majesty, its substance, its shape . . . it somehow ignores the mud huts and the pitiful palm groves.

He doesn't have the guts to get out of the car. He's still babbling. "Hiding on those stairs, for seventeen nights the waves beat against me and I waited for her. My friends in Tehran had arranged everything. We just had to get to Tehran. From there, we'd leave for Turkey. Why in the world did she stay? . . . To come out in bright daylight in the middle of that hellish square, for what?"

He climbs out of the car. Ever since he fell on his knees at the garbage dump, he seems to have no energy left in his legs to stand up straight. I put my hand under his arm to take him to the middle of the square, right where Kokab collapsed. To our right, the rubble of abandoned ruins; to our left, a mass of gray fog wafting in from the sea. He sits down and runs his hand over the dirt.

"The captain didn't demand that they punish Kokab. In a room, far from everyone, he just huddled down and stared at the wall. But his brother's rage was something else. It was he, Captain Safdar, who said you should both be stoned. You see, Captain Jalal didn't even come out the day Kokab died."

He smells the handful of dirt he has scooped up from the ground. He points to where Kokab was staring.

"What's there?"

"You mean what was there. Now it's just the ruins of Delvari's shop. A piece of the store sign is still sticking out of the rubble. Rusted, rotten . . . In the old days, it had a big painting of a Canada Dry bottle on it, with ice around it. Every time I saw it, my thirst . . . my mouth would water."

"What else is there?"

And I don't tell him that two stray dogs are sitting on what's left of the shop, watching us.

"She must have . . . Kokab must have come out for . . . They told me Kokab's eyes were riveted to this side of the square."

They have risen from the sea, the shadows drifting along the shoreline. Like people who refuse to approach each other, people who refuse to look at each other, they are standing farther away than they should . . . out of stones' reach. Something is happening that has never happened before, something we have never seen before. Even a child can sense when there's a new horror in the air. Kokab has sneaked out of the house. But even under a chador, that figure is unmistakably hers. An old woman ululates, she points at her and jeers, "Look, it's Lady Kokab! Virtuous Kokab . . ." From the other side, a woman screams, "Hussy! The shameless hussy has come out in bright daylight." Kokab freezes in the middle of the square. The wail of ululations grows louder. . . . I see people coming from every direction, from every doorway. . . . They're circling around Kokab. . . . Every way she turns, people block her path. Captain Jalal's brother has run out of the house. "Where do you think you're running off to, you contemptible wench?" . . . He's the one who throws the first stone. He calls out a benediction to God. The stone misses Kokab. It falls close to the men standing on the other side; it rolls up to their feet. The ululation of hundreds of women cuts through the air; it provokes the men. Captain Safdar's second stone misses, too. He shouts a few curses and moves closer. He hollers and let's fly yet another one. His eyes look like they're brimming with tears. This one hits Kokab on the head. Blood doesn't show on her chador. Blood on black fabric just glistens under the sun.

The earth and the sky are in a terrifying way. The circle of people is growing denser; closing in. They're still emerging from their huts. . . . Me, small and skinny, I'm being shoved around, pushed back. I scramble between their legs and make my way to the front. Captain Safdar shouts, "Only the nonbelievers will not throw stones" . . . and he throws a stone.

Suddenly, a whirlwind from the direction of the power plant, twisting and turning, lands in the middle of the crowd. Maybe it was Kokab herself who wanted to give her chador to the wind. Her infernal hair, exposed, caked with blood . . . that golden flame and the deep red of blood have together created an otherworldly color. . . . The crazed sun. People's sweat drips on my face. . . . The old women start. Here and there, flinging small stones that gently fall short of Kokab.

She's still standing tall . . . standing there more stubborn than the devil himself. And I see her turn in my direction. Her eyes quickly find me. She looks at me . . . questioningly. She looks at me.

Far away, the clouds on the horizon still glow red from a sun that sank into the sea some time ago. The hateful minutes pass slowly. He has planted his knees on the soil of Seven Captains. He seems to have given his life and energy to his eyes. He is staring in the direction of Delvari's store. I want to shout, You louse, there's nothing there but wreckage and carcasses of stray and diseased dogs.

"Why did she come out in broad daylight?"

Insolence! Insolence! That's what it was. Kokab, fueling the flames of rage. Defying all of us, mocking all of us, or perhaps out of spite for all those men, she swings her head to the left, to the right, and back . . . as if she's sitting in front of a mirror, fanning out her lavish hair . . . bloodied strands, like the snakes of hell. Perhaps it's the obstinate whorish flirtation that drives people to instinctively reach down for rocks and lumps of dirt. The voice of the captain's brother is no longer alone. . . . Kokab's eye bursts.

I don't know how much time has passed. . . .

"You could come and go as you wished in the captain's house. How much did you see of her?"

I have been dreading this question since the first moment I saw him.

"Once you were found out, everyone and anyone

who had ever seen you in some corner started talking,
started telling, even exaggerating."

"But you had given her my message. Why did she
confess? Why didn't she come?"

"I don't know. She wouldn't eat, she wouldn't speak.
Not one word. No matter how much the captain's
mother and sister beat her, they never heard a single
word or groan from her. Then one day, it was like she
suddenly broke. She stood in front of everyone and told
them everything. Places you had sneaked off to . . . The
old women said, you spent an entire night together on a
boat, you had gone out to sea. She had told them, from
start to finish, everything you had done. . . . Everything."

"No! Never . . . A boat? . . . We were never on a
boat together."

"It was like she had thrown shame and modesty to
the wind. She told them about all the times you had
been intimate, together."

"Could she have escaped from that room?"

"How would I know? I didn't see her toward the end.
In the early days, I would take her food. She wouldn't
eat it. . . . After that, I stopped. The old women themselves would give her something to eat."

He tries to stand. . . . He falls.

"Could she have run away?"

"Rooms have windows . . . don't they? Every hell-
hole has a window, did you know that? All hellholes
have windows and they all open from the inside."

And in the evening's twilight, all around us ghosts with their mouths open in a scream.

"They open easily from the inside. They even open in the middle of the night. When a clueless captain is fighting waves and typhoons and coast guards in the middle of the sea, slaving like a dog to get another wretched load of cargo to port, the window in the poor cuckold's happy house opens, and someone jumps out and goes to her whoring rendezvous. . . ."

His clenched fists punch through the air, trying to reach me. They don't.

"What's troubling you?"

"Do you actually understand other people's troubles?"

The wind . . . the wind . . . my scream and specks of my raging spit, on his face.

"Even back then when you had eyes, you couldn't see. Your eyes were only after other people's women . . . all for the thrill of a fuck."

"You've got filth in your head. Your head is full of filth. All you've got in there is cock's scum. Your head is so choked with shit that you don't understand what love—"

"Stop yakking, motherfucker. Your sleaze so opened the eyes of that innocent kid that I will never again—"

"It wasn't sleaze! It was love. Sleaze is what's in your head! . . . If it hadn't been love, Kokab would never have accepted it. It was love that ruined us. If it wasn't, it would have stayed hidden, like a thousand other lecheries."

I have no energy or breath left in me.

"After that, I never trusted a woman. I could never look at one of these virtuous Kokabs and not remember. Every time I thought of marrying a girl, I saw her with her legs open under a jackass. . . . I would jolt awake, choking on my vomit."

I stare into the blindness of his eyes to tell him, to tell him that the jackass I saw was always him . . . and I don't.

The shadow of the dogs is no longer on the heap of rubble. But I hear their howl far away in the night.

"Even as a kid you were sly. . . . You lied to everyone."

I grab at him. His frailty frightens me. . . . I let go. He sprawls out on the ground. He claws at the earth, earth that only the rain has dared wash of Kokab's blood and flesh. The screams of people hurling stones whirl around us. Someone shouts, "Wait, you infidels!" And the stones wail through the air. "Don't hit her anymore!" And this voice, too, is lost among the screams. And the stones wail through the air. . . .

He starts sobbing at my feet. "All these years . . . I always wondered. Now I'm sure. It's impossible for the captain to have suspected your pocket for no reason. You lied. . . . It was you who showed him the pearl."

"You got it right, but you got it too late, you louse. If you weren't such a bastard, you should've come out of your hole. You should've had the guts to face Captain Safdar and tell him it was your fault. If they killed you, maybe they wouldn't have spilled Kokab's blood. . . . Why didn't you come out?"

The wind . . . it carries away his sobs.

"I was sure she would run away. *Gillyflower* was code for our meeting place, you son of a bitch! She knew that *gillyflower* meant where she should go, where I would be waiting for her, when she should come. . . . She should've come. Night after night I waited for her."

I don't know whether I should tell him now or wait until he's on his deathbed. Time and time again I have seen it in my mind. When he's breathing his last breath, I bring my head close to his and whisper that I never gave his *gillyflower* message to his Kokab . . . that every time I went to her room, Kokab's eyes, staring at me, were desperately waiting. . . . If there was no message, she must have thought all that talk of love and devotion was a lie, that some bastard had just had his way with her and gone off. . . . And now . . . now that she has come out in the middle of the square, she has come to look for me . . . even under the hail of stones, she has glued her eyes on me. She is still waiting to see if there is a message. She's waiting for me to give her the message so that she can at least die happy. She wants to read it in my eyes, but she can't.

In the darkness of the night, not like the scattered camphor-colored lights of the mud huts, but clustered and white, the lights of the power plant lavishly glow by the sea. It looks like an ocean liner has sailed too close to the shore.

If You Didn't Kill
the Cuckoo Bird

YEARS HAVE PASSED SINCE THAT DAWN; I believe eleven years, eleven years from one moment. Yet I remain in prison, deprived of any manner of free will and happiness, and what's more, I have been forgotten. He had no one, and now I am the sole inheritor of this dispossession. I wish I had a photograph of him or, to put it more realistically, of myself, from those lost times. It is not important for me to know which of us had a finer face; rather, a photograph in these confusing times can reveal much that has been forgotten or that has nestled in the wrong folds of the mind. There are memories in my mind that I am no longer sure are my own personal experiences.

Nine years is not a short time. I will disregard the first few months as an occasion for us to find each other amid the crush of alienation and for our inevitable friendship to form. The oldest memory of him that remains in my mind belongs to the recreation hours outdoors. In single file we would walk in a small circle surrounded by gray walls, our pace imposed by a collective in which none of us played an independent role. Still, in the midst of our same-colored clothes, our common smell, and our exasperating lack of individuality, the stateliness of his movements and eyes that instilled an unpleasant yet irresistible sensation in any observer made him stand out. As the circle of flesh turned and the familiar sounds of rustling clothes and scraping heels spilled over the small yard, I would involuntarily watch him. Depending on where in the circle we were on a given day, different angles of his face and figure would be visible to me. And then we became cellmates.

He hated snoring—as I do now—and among all those men, I was the only one who did not transform my dreams and nightmares into hoarse rasps in the crater of sound, and it was this that led to our coming together and his acceptance of me. Yet, there were times when we—he and I—in the blistering and leaden air of rage, would go at each other simply to quench our thirst for social interaction and fresh associations. When we beat each other—in silence, so the night guard would not notice—we would swallow our groans. Fists are silent, especially if they land on the abdomen. Those in neighboring cells who became aware of our fights, with their shoulders shaking from stifled laughter and in anticipation of the gibes with which they would grace us the next day, would crawl under their blankets and from time to time listen to the muted fleshy sounds coming from our cell. His fists were heavier than mine. When he punched me, my breath would freeze in my chest and I would hunch over and press my arms against my sides. Then, after air gradually penetrated the constriction lodged under my sternum, I would rise up again and strike him. I would grind insults between my teeth and pound my fists against any organ within my reach. When we grew weak and drained, we would collapse on our beds; it was then that we could talk.

During the monotonous prison nights, the mind, like a night crawler, emerges from its lair and begins to hunt. It hunts for every movement, sound, or even abstract instinct that will nourish it so that it can then slither into the cavities of the distant past. Of course, that is only on nights when at dawn they are not coming to take someone to be executed. On such nights, the silence of the cellblock grows deeper. Everyone stares at the ceiling with wide-open eyes. Sleep, filled with fantasies of sprawling meadows, of the winter-morning sun shining on crystalline surfaces, and of beautiful, docile women with longing in their eyes, flutters overhead like a weary bird that wants to land on a branch swaying in the wind but cannot. And we obstinately resist this pleasant sleep so that when at last we surrender to it, it will be all the more enjoyable. And then it is dawn and the footsteps of those who come, and we are one man fewer.

The game—a term he used so as to conceal the inner savagery of our pastime—was the only means by which we could pass through those tall walls. He taught me to play. The rules were simple. Yet, without exaggeration, we both suffered to master it. The game would embrace us like a magic cocoon; it would spin time around us. And inside the dark and musty warmth of this spun filament, the game would transform us from larvae. Fluttering our wings, we would emerge, someplace else. . . .

During the first five of the nine years that we spent reflecting each other like mirrors, we shared our pasts, our memories, and our thoughts, often filling in exact details that came to us at later times. Over and over again. At first, we would drift along the ordinary and even dull exterior of our minds. Swimming and floating in a shallow pond where the feet reach the bottom and repugnance from the touch of silt and algae stains the point of contact. Commonplace memories of mundane relationships. We had plenty of time, so we crossed the pond. On its surface, the mysterious reflection of moonlight and the shadows of silvery young leaves lay before us. He would say, "Have you ever swum naked in the water? We are there now; it tickles. One must imagine it." Gradually, with nervous tension and taunts, the unveiling of secrets and the thrusting of humiliation's dagger into that ungual bulwark we call identity, we floated free in our abyss. It was vast.

Despite his claims to the contrary, we all knew there was no freedom for him. A three-hundred-year sentence, regardless of the various opportunities that would qualify him for clemency, would claim his entire life. Yet now he has gone—no, it is more accurate to say "escaped"—just as he had always promised he would, a claim that had often put him in the position of being ridiculed by others. At the time, he was forty years old, but now that eleven years have passed and I have turned

fifty-one, he is in possession of my youth. This intensi-
fies my feelings of having been cheated. To have years
of one's natural life span taken away in a single night
is not an insignificant loss to bear. Of course, I did
not face this fact with my current composure. I shouted—I won't deny that at first it was out of horror—and
then, when perforce I faced the dreadful reality, it was
out of rage and as testimony to what had happened.
The prison psychiatrist—here they have psychiatrists,
too—diagnosed my behavior as nothing more than
the result of an illness I had feigned to gain sympathy
and to pave my way to the prison infirmary for a break.
Our exchange lasted only a few minutes, after which he
threw me out so that the next patient, a madwoman,
could lie down on the bed and allow him to lay the eggs
of his inculcations in her mind like a cuckoo bird.

The details of what took place are as significant to
me as any personal memory or memento of the past
is to an individual. To avoid extinction or perhaps
the disarrangement of my past, I tell my current cellmate all that I recall of my life, recollections that I am
sure belong to me, and he commits them to memory:
the date of my birth, the town where I was born, my
father's name, lists of places and times that are of personal importance.

When the cellblock lights are turned off and that
particular prison silence, softer and colder than our
blankets, wraps around the corridors, stairways, and
lower floors, amid the hum of hushed moans and hallucinations in sleep, of the guards making their rounds,

and, later, of the yawns of the steel poles and doors contracting, digesting in the belly of this silence, I lie on my bed, close my eyes, and try to imagine a bright spiral at the point where my left and right visions meet. The spiral spins and splatters light; it widens; it moves closer and its brightness blankets the darkness in my eyes—the dazzling brilliance of a sunny day as I walk back from school. The warmth of the sun penetrates my skin and the hidden layers and cavities of my body; a numbness indicative of well-being creeps into my hands and feet. Our front yard had a fence separating it from the street. Ivies had coiled around its rusted bars and, half-grown, had dried up. They had strangled each other. I stand in the middle of the yard. I sense that the house is empty, void of life and deserted for years. The sharp angles of the building, its collapsed sections, and the height of its windows and the color of their curtains are unfamiliar to me. Have I been here before? I know this is a crucial moment. If I enter, my action will have forever chosen me and this house. Now I am inside the house. Someone is knocking, pounding an unyielding fist on the rusted steel. Nowadays, I can't bring sounds to life in my mind, perhaps because sound is the most perishable trace of our existence. There are pleading cries behind the door and that man walks out of his room. He casts a reprimanding look at me and cautiously opens the door a crack. Someone wants to enter and pushes against the door, claws at it, and the man bars the door from opening with his shoulder. Then I hear a scream and catch a glimpse of a woman through the narrow opening. The pressure of the door against her cheek has distorted her face. The man shouts, "Get lost, you double-crossing whore."

Now it's nighttime. When the doors in the cell-block slam shut, their unrelenting echo sounds famil-iar to me. Perhaps that door closed with this same sound. And then there is silence and a clump of that woman's hair remains stuck in the door, so that it can later be disposed of. I was able to recognize the face that, contorted from pain, fear, and tens of other emo-tions, had for an instant looked through the narrow opening in the door. She saw me. She was shocked—perhaps that is why she weakened and was pushed back. It was her, my mother.

He would ask, "Was it wintertime?"

I would not open my eyes. The sun would revolve in the spinning spiral and silvery waves would ripple high above the rooftops. It was wintertime, I'm sure: The memory of the winter sun shining on a faded fence and a garden patch with flowers is enduring. No, there were no flowers; that garden patch never had any flowers; it had a thicket of dry weeds and ivies that had woven their way through the fence.

"You passed the garden patch; the ground was tiled. Then there were the stairs; the edges of the stone steps were worn."

"Then there was the front door of the house, with flaking white paint."

"That had a brass handle."

"And in front of the door there was a metal screen; did you forget?"

"And when you entered, there was the hallway that was always dark."

"Most of the time. During the day, it had no sun, and at night, its lamp . . . I don't know. I don't remember its ever having a lamp."

"When was this? Exactly when? How old were you?"

"Twelve, thirteen, around then."

"And she was your mother."

"I saw her, her eyes, the color of her hair. There was a strange look in her eyes."

"So she wasn't dead."

"Dead?"

"You said before that she died before you started school. You spoke of her funeral; you remembered the white flowers and the black clothes. She taught you the names of the different colors."

I would shout, "She was not dead! No, that woman was my mother. I'm sure."

"She was your mother and she was not dead. You did not witness her death. Then she should still be alive, and even that father whom you despised."

"He despised me. He couldn't stand the sight of me. He wanted to kill me. I told you. He took me to the edge of the cliff and told me to look down. I looked down. I was terrified. I turned around and saw his hands ready to push me. I ran, and he called me.

He called me and ran after me and I ran faster. It was windy, raining; the tall weeds kept twisting around my ankles."

"This must be one of those dreams you wanted to have but never did; you just wanted to so that they would feel sorry for you like they would for a puppy."

"I didn't need that."

"A helpless little puppy caught in the midnight rain."

"So that I could hide my ugliness, just like you. So that I could make little girls cry and then flirt with them when they took my hand to comfort me."

That uniform brightness is no longer behind my eyelids; darkness has come. I open my eyes and half rise. He is still lying on his bed with closed eyes and confident breaths.

"You broke the rules of the game, stupid. You lied. Lies that you have always spun for yourself you are now spinning for me."

I would get up and beat him. Fists are silent. He would claw at my hair in the dark and throw me against the wall. I told you that he was big and strong. He took care of himself, always exercised, and when others would wake up in the middle of the night and masturbate, he would make fun of them. We shouldn't empty ourselves; energy must be preserved. He would exercise, wildly and with some deliberate masoch- ism, and then, exhausted and drenched in sweat, he would fall onto his bed. The strong smell of his body would flood the cell. And by the time he had caught his breath, his eyes would be closed and he would be imagining that bright spiral spinning around and filling the darkness behind his eyelids.

He would sprawl out like a drop of oil that drips onto a pool of water and blossoms with the one-dimensional rainbow that appears when light glides over a greasy film: greens, yellows, and reds that are inseparable, borderless. And then the lines would appear—glassy lines that were visible from behind one another and reflected on one another. The lines would connect and create faces and objects. Together with his voice, which like the squealing of the mice scurrying across the cement floor would creep into every corner and cavity of the cell, the contours of his words would pour into my eyes and create images. Whatever he saw, I saw. Him, as an eight-year-old, a thirteen-year-old, and then, later, his entire life. And by the time we had finished recounting our lives, that which had been private had become public—a shared ration ready to be remasticated and remade by trivial inaccuracies and personal perceptions. From then on, memories that once depended on my existence would reconstruct themselves in my mind, as though they had found an independent existence through him and his interpretations. They gained this ability during the final years of my first sentence and at a time when I was growing more tense and nervous by the day. How slowly time passed when I focused on the seconds. And when she would come, when she could, with a few flowers, time would pass even more slowly. At night I would speak of her during our game, of the words that her eyes had spoken after the guard in the meeting room had yelled, "Time's up!" Standing in the doorway, she would turn and look at me; she would push the cascade of her thinning hair behind her ear and her eyes would become her entire face, and her eyes would be all words, and the moment she was gone, I would crush the flowers in anger.

I close my eyes.

He asks, "Is she beautiful?"

"To me, very much so."

"It depends on one's taste."

"Yes."

"The flowers are from the garden at her house. All that distance. She gets on the train holding the flowers and comes."

"There is a willow tree in one corner of her garden."

"She wears dark clothes. Ever since you ended up here, you have never seen her wear brightly colored clothes, the ones that women fancy, that make them look like flowers."

"No, she doesn't. But she always wears her gold necklace. She leaves it hanging outside of her dress. I bought it for her. A bird in flight, on her chest."

"You think the most beautiful birds are golden."

"And there are none. There is no golden bird in the world other than hers."

The two bright dots of her pupils appear in the center of my eyes, but now they are opaque. A gray light spawns from the black, from the grayish black—fruit of an ancient contrast. And the cloudy color of a rainy day, the color of dawn on the sea's horizon, forms in my eyes. The sand is wet. It rained the night before and ours are the only footprints on the sand.

"I said, 'We will get married on a rainy day so that we can come here when there's no one around.'"

"Her voice. Did you say her voice is delicate?"

"Like the chime of an exotic Oriental instrument. Although I can't hear it now. I'm incapable of imagining voices."

"It is gray everywhere."

"I told you: Everywhere, the rain is waiting in the sky."

"I see it. You took her hand."

"But first she blew on her hands. They were ice-cold. The waves come close to our feet and I take her hand in my hands. My hands are warmer."

"You had given her the gold bird the day before; you wanted to say it, but you couldn't; you were afraid."

"I was afraid that maybe it was just a long dream, that if I said it, it would turn into mist, until the next day, when I just blurted it out."

"You said, 'We will get married on a rainy day so that we can come here when there's no one around.'"

"No. I said, 'When there's no one here and we can come.'"

"She laughed."

"She didn't get angry. She looked at me and laughed. Then she blew on her hands because of the cold and I took her hand, and together we watched the fog looming over the sea. If she hadn't agreed, she would have pulled her hand away and asked that we leave. We didn't leave. She said, 'I want to sit on the sand.'"

"The sand was cold and wet."

"But we sat down, facing the sea, and the fog that didn't rise from the water but instead descended from the clouds on the horizon glided in on the surface of the sea. Like a dancer on ice wearing a white lace dress."

The fog closes in on us. I get up and sit on my bed. My head is about to explode. Sweat is streaming down my temples. The air feels heavy and an old stale fog has swept across the cell. He says, "Let's go all the way to the end. It's not over yet."

"I can't. My head . . . My head is about to burst."

"You didn't let go of her hand, and when you sat down, you kissed it and squeezed it. She was looking out across the sea, at the dancer gliding toward you on one leg, with open arms and a smile as wide as her face."

"I wanted to kiss her lips. I leaned forward, toward her smooth, damp hair. Her perfume and the scent of the sea had mingled in it. She pulled her head back and said . . . she said . . ."

"'When we get married.'"

"Yes, 'When we get married, on a rainy day when there's no one here. Until then . . .'"

"She didn't say anything else."

"She laughed. . . . The air is so heavy; I have to splash some water on my face. I'm burning up."

"What else, after her laughter?"

I shouted. I shout, "No!"

I don't remember if she said anything else, and then we left, and . . . It is so warm. I feel like I'm suffocating. I get up and walk toward the door to call the guard. He is lying motionless on his bed and the reflection of a pale light, the source of which I cannot see, glides over his sweaty forehead and into the hair on his temples.

I tell my new cellmate, "This is how it was. Will you remember it?"

And in the dark, after he kept his silence all night long, I don't see him nod his head in confirmation. Sweating, I pace the length of the cell. In my mind, somewhere in the unreachable distant corners, lurks the fear of falling asleep and being robbed. The slightest movement or noise other than the usual nightly sounds wakes me up with a start and instantly a cold sweat lines my spine. I look around with wild eyes. The shadows, the glow of the night-lights, the footsteps of the guard moving away, and I think . . . What do I think? It's not important.

I believe our final night together bears as much weight as the entirety of those nine years. On that last night, I knew I would not be able to sleep. I lay staring at the ceiling like all the other men in the cellblock who, restless and secretly jealous of my happiness, tossed and turned in their beds, smoked and blew the smoke up in the air. And when silence frothed in the corridors, if I were to say anything, if I were to start the last round of the game, it would all be about her. And I would see her on a sunny day wearing a brightly colored dress and her golden bird, and I would fill the emptiness of all the years she spent waiting at the center of her life.

I got up and packed my things. All my belongings amounted to one duffel bag, which I placed at the head of my bed. I don't know why, but I felt depressed. His eyes secretly followed my every move, most of which were purely meant to kill time. I could have quietly hummed a common song, a song from years ago that people on the outside had probably long forgotten. I could have finished knitting my small pouch so that at the final moment I could offer it to someone as a memento. I had procured the yarn by unweaving a pair of old socks—in those days, this was customary in our cellblock. But I did none of these things. As I stood staring at my neatly made bed and that duffel bag, he said, "So you, too, are leaving."

I preferred not to speak. I didn't want anything to cloak the nakedness of those final moments. He went on: "She will definitely be at the prison gate tomorrow, waiting for you. With flowers and the golden bird on her chest . . ."

Then, with that same resentment and rage that would drive him mad whenever a prisoner was about to be released, he growled, "Someday soon, I, too, will escape from this prison, just as I have promised everyone."

"Make sure to look me up when you get out. You know where to find me."

He laughed. He understood my gibe and laughed and dropped down on his bed. He folded his hands under his head and stared at the ceiling. I had no patience for him. Perhaps because I knew he preferred that I remain in that cell with him for eternity, and in that damned leaden air walk behind him every morning in that circle and gaze at the tall walls and the guards' boots that stand on free ground. I said, "I will come visit you. I promise."

Again, he laughed. Perhaps he sensed sarcasm in my voice. Quietly, he said, "White cloud. The reflection of a patch of white cloud on the river."

I turned my back to him and moaned, I really moaned, "No!"

"The river's twenty-third autumn."

"Stop it!"

"When the cloud moved away from the sun, it went to stick to the mountaintop. Coins of light, silvery coins spread on the river, like the reflection of the sun on a slippery fish that has jumped out of the water . . ."

I stuck my fingers in my ears. I looked at my duffel bag; it was blue. I was waiting, waiting for the sound of steel doors to open one after the other and the heavy footsteps of the guard who would come, who would indifferently call out my name, and I would leave with him. I preferred to talk about something else, even, if he wanted, about women and our most private moments. I said, "Stop it."

"It was autumn."

I had closed my eyes. I felt dizzy. I wanted to walk so as to neutralize the effect of his words with the sound of my feet. I wanted to think of her, of the fluttering wings of the golden bird on her chest as she walked on a rainy day. I wanted to, but I couldn't. The sun, the sunshine in his mind penetrated my eyes. A yellow autumn sun reflecting on the leaves.

"You sat down. There, where the water was calm, it flowed gently and tiny dark fish aimlessly wandered after one another in the shallow waters. You thought, What a waste . . . The razor blade was in your pocket."

"No!" I shouted, but my voice drowned in the commotion of the cellblock. The time for silence had not yet arrived.

"You had come all that distance with a razor blade in your pocket. You must have taken it from in front of the bathroom mirror."

"No, I found it. I was holding it."

My palms were sweaty. It wasn't hot, but it wasn't cold, either; it was desensitized autumn weather, but I was sweating. The razor blade was wet in my hand.

"You see the sequins of light on the water. The water's gentle murmur fills your ears. You wonder why the river is not deep."

"It wasn't deep at any point; it flowed with a gentle slope."

"And it wouldn't have made a difference. You can swim. People who can swim can't drown themselves, unless they tie a heavy weight around their bodies and fill their pockets with rocks. Right? You thought . . ."

"I had found it, on the ground, like the symbol of an inescapable fate, and I had immediately thought, Why not . . . ?"

"You had already thought of it. That's why you'd come to the river. You said so yourself."

"Yellow, there was yellow everywhere, a yellow-and-burnt-crimson strip along the river's edge as far as the eye could see. I sat down."

"You thought about the drops of blood that drip into the water—they stretch and run in every direction. Thin red lines in the clear water that expand and disappear."

"The fish would have to escape. They hate blood, don't they?"

"I don't know."

Exhausted, I fall back on my bed; my eyes close. The sun shines on the razor blade. The left hand or the right hand?

"Do you think it was the left hand or the right hand?"

"I can cut better with my right hand. I bent back my left wrist so that the veins stuck out and I held it over the water."

"Funerals. They are the most conventional and comical ceremony we humans have. Those seemingly sad faces, hands that their owners don't know what to do with, and time that passes so very slowly."

I looked. It was my last look at the surfaces of life, the burnt red and yellow leaves, the sky that seemed deeper in the distance and of a darker blue, the river's bend, the patch of cloud that was floating toward distant mountaintops.

"The sounds. The sounds of life."

"There was a rustle, a faint rustle, in the trees, on the wet ground blanketed with leaves, and in the bracken fern plants. Perhaps I also heard the sound of a bird flapping its wings."

"Your hands were shaking. You thought, What if the razor blade is blunt? What if it only cuts the surface of the skin and . . ."

"I thought, Why not with electricity, wouldn't it be easier? Or plunging off a tall building so that I sprawl out in the middle of the street and all the cars have to brake."

"There they wouldn't find your body; it would stay and swell and decompose; your hand would fall into the river and you would collapse on the riverbank; the light would bother your eyes and the last of the red drops would fall free in the water. You were frightened, frightened of the loneliness of your corpse, of the last remnant of your existence being ravaged. . . ."

"No."

"You were frightened, frightened of death."

"It was useless."

"No it wasn't; it was fear."

"Death would have come on its own. Why should I have hurried it along?"

"No, you got scared; you probably thought life still had a few measly alms to offer that you could snatch up."

I drop the razor blade and I run.

"The razor blade floated for a few seconds; it glistened like the sides of a fish rolling in water and then it sank and you could no longer see it."

A branch was floating by. A hand had broken it off, spun it around, ripped that dreadful howl out of the air, and then carelessly thrown it in the river. I got up. I was drenched in sweat. Was it from fear? Or perhaps I really had changed my mind. Anyway, these reflections are now useless. Here, I am not threatened by any unexpected incident. Sometimes I think an earthquake and a subsequent fire may destroy the prison and all of us in it, but fortunately the walls and ceilings are so solid that they eliminate this possibility, too. Prison is eternal. I like the poetic nuance of this sentence and I sometimes repeat it to myself.

But I digress. I should instead carefully arrange the pieces of this confusing puzzle, starting with the outer edges and working my way in toward its center. At times I am incapable of such concentration. I have to strain my mind until the desired result—the truth—is revealed. I remember that, contrary to my expectations, he was not sad. When I looked at him, his eyes had their usual lively glint. His final reactions are of great importance to me because they are the only evidence with which I can prove that everything had been prearranged and that in no way did chance have a hand in this incident. In any case, I thought, Perhaps he is happy. I wanted to go to bed early that night. Sleep liberates us from time—a threadbare coat that we take off. He was quiet. I could feel the weight of his eyes—eyes that slyly kept me under watch. We lay down on our beds. I could smell the revolting stench of roach poison. I had grown accustomed to it years ago and no longer noticed it, but now my sensitivity to it had been revived. The same was true of the coarseness of the blanket that bore my scent, the squeaking of my bed, and the rustling of my clothes. And then we switched beds. He suggested it.

I stretched out on his bed and immediately sensed the strong smell and warmth of his body. I preferred to not say anything lest I reveal my excitement. When he started to speak, it seemed as though his voice were coming from someplace far away, far from me, from behind the bars, the steel doors, and the dark cement walls. He said, "Tomorrow, when you walk out of the gates, she will definitely be there."

"The last time she came, she said she would be there."

"With flowers?"

"Maybe."

He smirked. He always laughed mockingly when he was angry. Then, without warning, he asked that for our final game we move forward. I am not sure whether he used the word *forward* or *future*. And then he added, "to a destiny that exists only for you, things that you will do."

"We will get married, without delay."

"You're not going to wait for a rainy day?"

"I've been waiting for nine years. Tomorrow, perhaps, we will get married, and go to a place where there are no people around."

"She is standing there, I see her, wearing a brightly colored dress and the golden bird on her chest. You see her when the great gate closes behind you. Is she laughing?"

"I don't know. I walk toward her, or she will walk toward me. But first, I turn around and look back at the great gate and the walls. When they brought me here, I paid no attention to their other side. What color are they? How do they affect the colors outside? She will walk toward me, definitely."

"You walk toward each other. Will you hug her?"

"I think so. I want to."

I felt light-headed. The dense shadow of a deep and untimely sleep hovered in my head. I saw her. As far as I could remember, there was a wide street in front of the prison's main gate, and as she stood across the street, the passing cars etched lines across her image. Then she saw me and laughed. . . .

"If timidity permits. You are both good people, but after all this time . . . You kiss her. And then you think your smell bothers her. You move away from her."

"I take her hand and we run to get away from this place."

"Fresh air, sun, rain, lovemaking, and . . ."

Shimmering sparkles floated in my eyes. A sense of well-being coursed through my body, a sort of pleasant fatigue that craves stillness. Behind my eyelids the image of her smile became eternal, and then sleep, deep sleep, spread across my mind. That was the last time I saw her, but for a long time her voice continued to crawl around in my ears. And in the darkness that spread layer upon layer on the slippery surface of my eyes, the lines of light faded, and during a slow and endless descent, I heard confused sounds that no longer made any sense. And I thought, There is no escape from noise, not even in sleep. . . .

Time in a confined space has strange characteristics. Despite the sluggishness of its moments, some sort of speed and movement is concealed in its totality. These eleven years and all that has happened to me since his escape are now buried somewhere in the incredulity of my thoughts like the continuation of that night's sleep. To awaken from a sleep that is not substantiated by the presence of nightmares or dreams; and that mirror, that mirror with its rusty surface that has always been there, hanging on the wall. My new cellmate—given all that I have said, I will call him "new," although he has been with me for eleven years—continues to be surprised by my interest in the mirror. Perhaps he is even irritated by what he perceives to be my vanity. Although I have told him and continue to tell him the entire story—as I have told everyone—he has only pretended to believe me. But at least he has been consistent in his dishonesty. Despite my frequent and unwavering attestations, he, like everyone else, has not entertained the slightest doubt that perhaps I am telling the truth. They laugh—the most common human reaction when faced with realities that we do not have the capacity to accept. They all laugh, just as they did on that morning when I forced my face through the bars and yelled, "He has escaped!"

When I woke up from that deathlike sleep and glanced over at my own bed, I saw that he was not there. My duffel bag was not there, either—this I realized later. It was perhaps only moments after he had gone. My heart sank. I thought I heard the squeaking of the cellblock doors closing. I called the guard. I asked him why no one had come to release me. He laughed. Others who overheard me laughed, too, and then the entire cellblock laughed. I thought perhaps I had miscalculated the days. When I asked, "Where is he?" they laughed even harder. Imagine a prison filled with laughter. It is terrifying. And then I caught sight of the mirror.

The entire incident ends here. I still have not grown used to this body that has been imposed on me. It remains foreign to me because I have no memories and no personal reminders of its limbs. I look at it. I look all over this that represents a sentence in a different prison. I hate the smell of its sweat; I hate everything it excretes; I even hate its primal needs and habits. My sensibilities are not compatible with it, they resist it, and this constant friction produces restlessness and confusion in me. Yet I take good care of it. Just like him, I exercise it every day; I feed it when it is hungry, and when it gets sick, I attempt to cure it, as if it were my own body—the one that on that morning walked out of the prison gates and recognized her, waiting with flowers and the golden bird on her chest, and before walking toward her turned to look at the outside of the tall prison walls and planted the image of his smirk on them for more than three hundred years. And at that very moment I shouted, I recoiled in horror as his eyes stared back at me from the mirror. It was not me in the mirror; it was him, his face. . . .

My new cellmate wipes his sweaty forehead with his sleeve and, when I have no more to say, leans back on his elbows and mutters, "Perhaps he'll come visit you."

"He won't. He's afraid."

And I will not say why he's afraid. He stares scrupulously at the lines on my face and tries to detect spasms of insanity in them. But he will find nothing other than the wrinkles and gauntness of my lost years, years when he was older than I, years in which he alone had lived and I only know his memories of them, memories that I now share with my current companion. My cellmate has a good mind and has promised to remember everything that has to do with me, so that he can help me if one day I fail to distinguish myself in the two pasts that have formed in my mind.

At night, in the familiar silence of the prison, I fold my hands under my head; I close my eyes and talk. I know that if he doesn't think of the two years remaining in his sentence, if it is not his turn to speak, he will not be able to sleep, even if he is tired. His eyes will close and a shining spiral will appear in the darkness. The sun. It's a sunny winter day and I am walking home from school. . . .

Credits

"Shadows of the Cave," *AGNI*, vol. 87, 2018.

"Mummy and Honey," *Words Without Borders*, November 2010.

"Shatter the Stone Tooth," *Strange Times, My Dear: The PEN Anthology of Contemporary Iranian Literature*, Arcade Publishing, 2005.

"Seasons of Purgatory," *The Literary Review*, Fall 2007.

"If She Has No Coffin," *CONSEQUENCE* magazine, vol. 7, Spring 2015.

"King of the Graveyard," *The Kenyon Review*, vol. 34, no. 2, Spring 2012.

"The Color of Midday Fire," *EPOCH*, vol. 60, no. 3, 2011.

"Seven Captains," *The Kenyon Review*, vol. 31, no. 3, Spring 2009.

"If You Didn't Kill the Cuckoo Bird," *The Virginia Quarterly Review*, Summer 2010.

Bellevue Literary Press is devoted to publishing
literary fiction and nonfiction at the intersection
of the arts and sciences because we believe
that science and the humanities are natural
companions for understanding the human experience.
We feature exceptional literature that explores
the nature of perception and the underpinnings
of the social contract. With each book we publish,
our goal is to foster a rich, interdisciplinary dialogue
that will forge new tools for thinking
and engaging with the world.

To support our press and its mission,
and for our full catalogue of published titles,
please visit us at blpress.org.

Bellevue Literary Press
New York